This issue arrives with the first breath of spring. The first thaw, perhaps. Definitely in time for that first kiss—that first blush of awareness. This issue contains stories about what we hold on to after love leaves us, stories about who we wished we could be, stories about the terrible things that haunt us, and stories about the way the rest of the world is haunted. This issue is the one where we reveal the mask beneath the face we were wearing last year.

Don't be surprised. We're still the same on the inside.

Underland Arcana is published on a seasonal basis. This issue is published in conjunction with the spring equinox, as tiny leaves start to bud and ideas begin to blossom.

EDITOR
Mark Teppo

COVER IMAGE
Berit Kessler / stock.adobe.com

SIGIL ART
Andrew Penn Romine

PUBLISHER
Underland Press
Clackamas, OR, USA

The ice breaks. We trade one skin for another . . .

https://www.underlandarcana.com

UNDERLAND
ARCANA

~ 09 ~

Underland Press

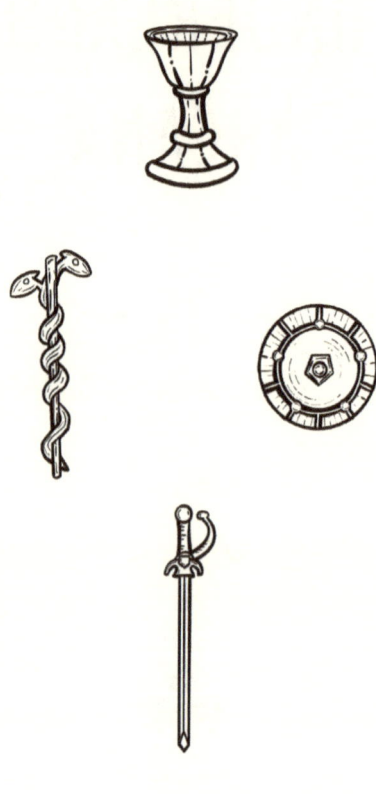

Contents

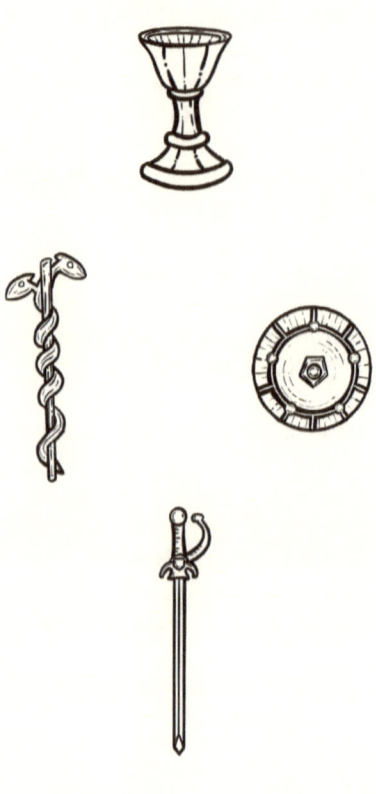

The Rise of Spring

We're experiencing a bit of a cold snap in the Pacific Northwest as I write this, which is to say temperatures hovering around freezing. The sky is clear. The nights are brisk. You can see the stars. The moon rises late, and none of us are there to greet it because we have gone a-hiding under the blankets with a hot water bottle. Yes, wrapped around our sloshy friend through the night, waiting for the sun to return. It will come back, won't it?

That's one of those quiet little prayers we offer, isn't it? How many of those have crept into our lives these last few years? More than you think. More than we'd like to admit. The quiet yearnings we allow ourselves during the night, under the cover of blankets with only the sloshy one as witness. In the morning, we pour that water out. Don't look too closely. It is streaked with our nighttime tears. Pour them out. Pour them into the dark cisterns and waterways that run beneath the earth. Where do they go? Some great lake of watery fears and nighttime tears that lies deepdark beneath our feet. What drinks from that lake?

Anyway, welcome to issue nine of Underland Arcana, the first issue of our third year. It's a bit of a milestone. We've been doing this long enough now that there is some routine, and there are enough issues that we can point at the archive and say, "Why yes, it reads like this." With this assurance—oh heck, let's call it confidence!—we thought we might start providing a little editorial note to accompany each issue. Some manner of explanation, if you will, but not so much as to divert your attention overlong from the stories. That is why we are here, after all . . .

I've been fascinated with the Tarot for a long time, and I certainly don't pretend that I am an expert in their regard. Barely a devotee, but surely an eager one, nonetheless. Like all occult objects, they are both more and less than they appear. You can put a lot of faith in them. You can make adorable little earrings out of them. You can use them to plot a novel (says the guy who has, on more than one occasion). In all cases, they reflect and reveal more readily than anything else. I love how they give us permission to make shit up, which is, frankly, the secret tool in every creative arsenal. That eternal response of "Yes, and . . ."

The standard marketing flap for Arcana runs like this.

> *Underland Arcana offers four aspects of this perpetual spark: the numinous, the esoteric, the supernatural, and the weird. These are the ways that hope manifests. These are the ways we keep ourselves engaged. These are the ways by which we learn how*

to fight monsters. We stand with cup, shield, sword, and stick. This is the iconography of Arcana. These are the four quarters of the whole. These are the ways we heal, harbor, howl, and hum.

Though it may be hex, herd, howl, and hum. I keep changing my mind. Regardless, the project has always been a bit of a moving target. Is it horror? Is it fantasy? Is it science fiction? The answer is "yes." It's also confounding and weird and experimental. Because these things need homes too, you know. And so, as we wander into the third year of Arcana, know that the project will keep changing its spots. It will learn to swim. It knows how to curl up into a ball. You can't scoop it, and you certainly can't dance to it.

By the way, with this issue, I now have a story in the Arcana archive for each of the Minor Arcana cards of the Tarot. This was a milestone I was waiting for.

Enjoy.

Mark Teppo
February 2nd, 2023

KING of PENTACLES.

(Im)Permanence,
A Short and Long Story

~ Fayaway & Hermester Barrington

a mockingbird's "Chaw!"
treefrog's prrrrreeeet Robin's panpipes
windowpane cracking

lightwaves and soundwaves
bounce from rippled lake's surface
rocking marriage bed

waterbed island
luna moth fay and satyr
we balance barefoot

carp or catfish leaps
great blue heron squawks and flies
we exchange our rings

"We do!" we both shout
jacaranda petals fall
"we do!" shouts the shore

kiss freezing spacetime
bat flies through cracked window
slips behind the frame

A sound of glass cracking—not dreaming anymore, she guesses, slipping from the now mostly still bed and running downstairs, Zoë chases something that flies into the library and slips behind their watercolor wedding portrait. In the alcove behind, she finds a marbled paper envelope. Inside, a letter in her own flowing script, addressed to her:

> *We had a dream last night, Zoë, and this year I think we should gather everything we've created this past year and hide it, or destroy it. I'm pretty sure that will work. I've talked about this with Robin, and he's already set everything up.*
>
> *And a very merry un-birthday to us both!*

Under her signature is a date—a year ago, tomorrow.

Wheels creaking behind her, she turns as Robin pulled her childhood wagon into the library. Embracing her before slipping her silk kimono over her shoulders—"I don't think you need it, but we should think of the neighbors," he said, then asked: "Are you ready?"

Nodding, she points about the room—"That one, that, and oh, god yes, that"—as he carefully piled into the wagon a Klein bottle containing a dancing Rebis, a Zen garden of hammered gold with a brass cricket chirping in the tree, and a shroud bearing Andy Warhol's likeness, along with a few other items.

"You should be the one to put these in, Zoë," Robin said, handing her a stack of notebooks and sketchpads.

"These are my workbooks, and my journals!" she cries, flipping past sketches of proposed projects—a lava lamp in a vintage Mountain Dew bottle, a chicken claw and human hand drawing each other, notes for a book on vespertiliomancy . . .

"A private archive has agreed to preserve them," Robin replied, "only carefully selected researchers may read them, and to protect us, no one may make copies or photographs until nine hundred and ninety-nine years have passed. I expect that they will be very popular!"

"Well, there's a lot of personal stuff here," she sighs. "But maybe whoever sees them will tell our story, someday." And she places them gently in the wagon, then begins pulling it to the garage to load up the Travelall, the wagon's shocks creaking.

Coming back into the library, Zoë finds Robin pulling a wicker burial basket into the center of the room. "I think I need to be alone for a while," she says, quickening her pace, striding out into the garden and toward the lake. Beyond the lawn, the wild grasses, still covered with dew, tickle her thighs.

She stops to gaze at the fountain in the center of the wild space—composed of shattered clay sundials, water sparkles cheerfully over its surface, and into the basin buried deep in earth, mallow and mustard, and moss. Mounds of earth covered in grass and wildflowers surround it, laid out like numbers on a clock face.

Humming, Robin pulled the creaking wagon behind him to a spot without wildflowers, and picked up a shovel. The blade cutting into the soil released the scent of moist earth into the late winter air. Inhaling those scents, Zoë picks up a spade to join him, and they soon have a good sized pit between them.

"Um, how long have we had this fountain, Robin? Didn't Jorge and Gabriela give it to us when they sold us this place?" Zoë asks as they dig.

Looking away, Robin replied, "Yes, it was their wedding gift to us, so we've had it about two and a half years."

"Only that long? It looks like it's been here longer than that."

"Plants benefit from love, Zoë, and so they grow faster here than anywhere else, I think," he said, laughter in his voice.

"Well, that explains it," she says, grabbing his ass and pulling him close for a kiss.

"I think later would be better, Zoë," Robin said, pulling away. "We should get this done, and we don't want these plants to get fat!"

"I'll hold you to that," she says, and so, smiling, they begin to dig again.

Zoë digs out a few more spadefuls as Robin pulled the wagon closer and slid the basket in. She lights the kindling underneath, uncertain whether the damp earth would extinguish the flame, which finally caught.

Through the willow withes comes the sound of clay cracking, metals melting, paper burning. She laughs as a single page with the word "Mitrúvishar" flies out on an updraft and sails into the lake, extinguishing itself with a hiss Zoë could not hear, and she wonders what that word might have meant to her. She tosses damp tissues into the flames as Robin filled in in the hole and scattered seeds on the ground, composing all the while:

> *the smell of turned earth*
> *and last years' artworks' ashes*
> *wildflowers planting*

"How many times have we done this, Robin?" she asks, looking at the other mounds, and Robin smiled, but said nothing.

"Mother Nature is watering the seeds," laughs Zoë, as they finish tamping down the soil, and she counts the rain drops until there were too many. After a supper of fruit, cheese, and wine inside, Robin and Zoë kiss good-bye on the front porch. "I'll be back before dawn," he said, and Zoë listens as the Travelall rattles down the road and onto the highway, going inside when the lake's silence returns with the dusk. Stretching out on the floor of the library with a copy of *The Bloody Chamber*, she smiles as she reads, for the nth time, of the Frog Prince rising up from Devil Reef to marry the Princess, whose children live happily ever after; a moment later, the book drops from her hand and her eyes close.

"Kakā-kakā-kakā!" rising from the lake awoke her, and she laughed—"Yes, I'll be rinsing and cleaning indeed, Ms. Duck!"—just before midnight; slipping out of her kimono, she gathers a few things and heads out to the deck. Settling in, she lights her opium pipe, the first of this year and the last of the next, and watches the ripples, wavelets, the slow movement of the waters toward the dam.

A truck gears down on the highway, and a duck quacks again. Out on the other shore, a frog croaks, several times, and then is silent. Bats fly in and out of the light's glow. Her pipe goes out as she rises, disrobes, and walks down to the lake.

"Cold!" she squeals, as mud squelches between her toes, lily pads brushing past her body, until she is up to her shoulders in the lake. Holding her birth certificate and her driver's license, the flames singe her fingers, until she plunges beneath the surface. Staying under until her head grows light, she floats free of the water weeds and kicks her way towards the shore.

Three glugs of amaretto pouring into a glass to warm her, she settles on the deck to fill out a request for a copy of her birth certificate and a new driver's license, adding one year to last year's birthdate. The asphalt, still warm on her bare feet as she walks to the post office, smells of the recent rain, and mixes with the aroma of algae from the lake. "Hah!" she shouts, as she slams the mailbox lid. "Twenty-five years old again this year!" A dog barks, and she laughs.

A screech owl calls out as she settles down at the lake's edge again; writing a letter to herself, she seals it and lays it aside, then listens as last year's pen and ink splash in the lake below. Taking a new dip pen and journal in hand, she begins to write.

thick white drifting smoke
clinging to journal pages
poppy petals bloom

my birthdate burning
my smiling picture melting
pair of loons wailing

wind guttering flames
water swirling around me
I duck under—shhh!

dip pen scratching self
into paperwork boxes
cold wind drying us

slamming mailbox shut
"hah!" I shout, "another year—
gone!" bare feet warm street

empty picture frame
still warm documents behind
mockingbird singing

dip pen scratching out
poems of the year just now born
wavelets on the shore

past years' leaves' shadows
pinned to the sycamore's bark
torchlight flickering

Venus to the east
melting into the sun's light
his feet on the stairs

This last haiku she hears as Robin read it to her, waking her gently from her sleep. Putting down her journal, he bent to kiss her. "Welcome home, Robin," she says, pulling him close, "I missed you last night," and Robin responded in kind. Moments later, in the garden, they feed the newly planted seeds on the mound, laughing as a car door slamming startles them. Rising together, she brushes the moist earth from his back as he returned the favor.

Zoë settles on the deck to watch the sun continue to rise; Robin, holding a canvas bag, sat beside her and picked up her new license—"Nice photo!" he said—then took out an empty picture frame, a pad of paper and Zoë's colored pencils. "I spilled water on our wedding portrait this morning," he said. "Could you please draw us another?"

"Yes—tell me what you remember about it, Robin—I'm so sleepy . . ."

"Well, it was just lovely. We married almost two and a half years ago, on . . ."—and Zoë writes the date across the bottom in her flowing hand, as he points out toward the center of the lake—"on the island, there. The wisteria and jasmine from the bower got us a little high, or maybe we were just in love—in any case, we couldn't stop grinning, and you giggled the entire time. You wore a bright green peasant blouse and olive skirt, a garland of hibiscus with your hair long. Luna moth wings sprouted from your back, and I . . ."

Zoë's hands move quickly as she sketches an outline for the watercolor. *I probably won't finish it today,* she thinks, *guests are coming at dusk for the party, and there is a lot to do before then, but we have time—we have always had time now.* Robin's voice guiding her hand, she smiles as he recalled for her, as if it were yesterday, a fish leaping at the moment they shout "We do!" a raven watching them from the sycamore, their words echoing from the lake shore, some crepe myrtle blossoms, blown by the breeze, showering onto them as they kiss as if for the first time, again . . .

Voyeur; or, Helen of Troy, the Most Beautiful Woman in the World

~ Daniel David Froid

Ernestine told me she had just returned home from her travels. "*Just*," she said. "Got back this morning and I haven't even unpacked."

We sat inside her grubby kitchen, at a table piled high with junk. I glanced at my sister across the landscape formed by a few weeks' worth of mail, a pot full of soapy water, another, lidded pot, made of enameled cast iron in pink, several bottles of vitamins and pills, and a couple of boxes of food, with crackers in one and cookies in the other. The boxes were closed, and no food was on offer. A small patch of space had been cleared in one corner. I made a mental catalogue of all this accumulated junk while she moved around the kitchen, making coffee. Her house, in a state of unnerving disorder, could not be blamed on her extensive travels but on her regular habits, ever feeble, as a housekeeper.

She poured a cup of coffee for each of us and sat down. Cheryl, her dog, an elderly Vizsla, brushed past us before perching on a bed in the corner. She—Cheryl—had one in every room.

Ernestine was telling me she had once again gone to the Furono system. "At least that was the plan," she said. Lately, whenever she returned from one of her trips, she would call me and insist that I visit. Dutifully, I always did; I suppose some shred of sororal devotion lingered on in me. She never used to call me at all, until she had, in her retirement, taken up traveling. Or what she referred to as traveling. I'll admit that I could never quite say whether, or to what extent, I believed her. And yet, after so many years of silence, silence that at times felt vaguely menacing, I welcomed her gesture. I listened with tolerance to stories I scarcely believed. They seemed to me not far off from the stories she fabricated in our youth, stories in whose telling I once partook, full of magic and secrets, incantations we whispered in the dead of night in the forest just behind the house.

As she spoke, my mind flashed to the face of our brother, who did not like her stories, who did not like to play; quickly, I cut him out of my mind and turned to Ernestine.

"That far?" I asked. "I'm impressed."

Ernestine chuckled and lit a cigarette.

"Furono's not my favorite, but I got a good deal. And it's not so far, you know. Just one system over. But then I ended up going to Videro, and *that* is a place worth seeing."

While Ernestine spoke, Cheryl glanced at us with a look I can only describe as beatific: eyes narrowed, gazing toward the heavens and waiting to receive a sign from God. She often looked this way, and I wondered how often she received such signs in return. About as often, I thought, as her human companion traveled among the stars.

I smiled and sipped the coffee, which was rich and strong. In Videro, the coffee is expensive but very fine—or so Ernestine says. I had never been myself. I asked, "This is good. Is it Videran coffee?"

Ernestine smirked. "Yes indeed."

"But is it actually coffee?" I asked and looked down at the thick, dark liquid, which swirled thickly when I tilted the cup back and forth. "It just occurred to me to wonder. Are we actually talking about the same plant here? I mean, we can't be."

Ernestine tutted. "You have such a narrow mind. There are only so many elements in the universe, you know. Here we have a composition that is as close as anything you'd like. Closer than some swill I've had on Earth in my time." Her mug was already empty, and she rose to refill it. Mine remained nearly full.

"Well. Okay then. Tell me about the trip."

"The plan," she said. "was to stay in Furono. I had to leave because everything moves too slowly there. And I can't stand the people. Perhaps I shouldn't say that, but it's true. They all sit around and have these lengthy, abstract conversations about what it means to exist. I mean, this is dinner table conversation. This is what they discuss with their kids! There was this little girl in the hotel where I was staying. . . . My first morning, I sit there

sipping my coffee and eating some very good pancakes—
and yes, pancakes, even if they were not made of good
old earth flour and eggs and whatnot." She raised a finger
at me and jabbed it, once, decisively, before continuing:
"And this girl comes up to me, and she asks me my name
and I tell her, and I ask her hers. It seems like a perfectly
pleasant interaction, and I tell her she seems like a very
nice little girl, and then she says, in this lisping little-girl
voice, 'Is my niceness your perception or is it a true quality of mine? Is it an essential quality of my being?' She
went on like that, about the inherent nature of qualities,
for a few minutes—minutes that felt, I am telling you,
like hours. And at last I simply excused myself to use the
bathroom and fled to my room. I could not bear it."

"She was trying to make conversation," I said, "in the
only way she knew how." My coffee had lasted for this an-
ecdote's duration, and, now my cup was empty, I wanted
more. I stood up, prompting Cheryl to bark, weakly. She
lifted her head from its pillowed recline, said her piece,
and then let her head drop.

"Forgive her," Ernestine said. "She doesn't like sudden
movements. Not at her age." She laughed and said, "I
don't either." After a pause, she continued, "I personal-
ly cannot bear the tedious philosophical speculations of
others; I do not care one whit!" Ernestine scrunched up
her face in disgust.

"You know who questions like that remind me of," I
said. My sister's face changed, from disgust to a darker
emotion. Something flashed in her eyes. I was the one

who said it, yet suddenly I did not want to grant that who a referent. "Our little brother," I whispered. Pursing her lips, looking away from me, Ernestine said nothing. My cup full once more, I returned to my seat.

"Anyway," Ernestine said, "when I was there, I heard all about this new interstellar liner that would be swinging by before moving on to Videro. *The Voyeur.* It was another guest at the hotel who told me, this very tall and very thin hairless man whose name I can't remember. But he was a human, and quite pleasant, and he said he knew the owner and could get me a discounted ticket. Now, I did not fall off the turnip truck yesterday, Cloris, and ordinarily a bland and pleasant man with such an offer would give me pause. To say the least."

"I would say so."

"Yes. Ordinarily the offer of a trip past the edge of the system, on a ship called *The Voyeur* no less, would be a sign that I should turn tail and run all the way home." Now she stood up, walked to the fridge, and paused to look back at me. "Are you hungry? I'm starved."

I demurred with a shake of the head. She busied herself, gathering things—eggs, a green pepper, an onion—to fix herself something to eat.

She said, "So I may have been tempted to see my way out. To flee. Whatever. And yet. What can I say? The devil of curiosity overtook me, and it prompted me to ask him to say a little more. And he did, he went on about how fabulous *The Voyeur* is. He said, 'Anything you'd like to take a peek at, you can, if you pay for the pleasure.'

And, anyway, everyone says that Videro will dazzle you. The most spectacular sight in the galaxy." She paused mid-chop, one hand clutching a knife and hovering over an onion. "A spectacular sight: is that redundant, Cloris? I think it is. Spectacle is inherent to any sight. Or, better: to be worthy of being seen is inherent to a spectacle."

"Careful, Ernestine. You're beginning to sound like the little girl from Furono."

Her eyes glowed; she barked out one singular laugh. "The beaches—in colors you've never even dreamed. The cities—as tall as the sky. So he said, and I began to believe him, or perhaps it was only that my travels had left me dazed and debilitated. Interstellar journeys take a lot out of a woman, you know."

What was there to do but wait, patiently, for her to continue? That these tales seemed to me mendacious has already been noted. The extravagant telling of tales has long been a passion of Ernestine's—her whole life long. The first time she told me she had just returned from a journey beyond our solar system, I decided neither to argue nor to question her but to take her at her word, just to see what would happen, to see how she would proceed. With plentiful details and a coherent narrative thrust, her tale at least amused me if it did not altogether convince. As then, so now. If what she offered were lies, I accepted them anyway. Now, I waited. Cheryl rustled the blankets as she shifted her slumbrous body. Eggs sizzled in a pan that rested above flames of blue and white. My sister banged the pan against the stove and cursed. I pictured her, sitting glumly on a rocket that rattled through the cosmos, white fire trailing behind it. In my mind, Ernestine in her ratty housecoat, cigarette in one hand, straddled the rocket like a pinup girl riding a bomb as it shot across the sky, smirking and waggling her fingers at me in a patronizing wave.

"And so I went. I boarded *The Voyeur*." She sat down, soon, eggs fried hard and doused in hot sauce, the edges crisp if not burnt, and for a long moment she wielded the fork as though she were about to conduct an orchestra.

"That guy, I lost him. I didn't need him anymore. He seemed like a bit of a shady character, however useful I found his tips. The ship itself was grand. Not a rocket, sister, but a proper starship, enormous, equipped for deep-space flight, and painted the most beautiful shade of red."

"How did you know I imagined a rocket?"

"The wide and deep grooves of familiarity, worn into the paths that a mind daily treads, may occasionally be mistaken for telepathy."

"Ah," I said, and felt faintly embarrassed as the image of Ernestine straddling the rocket flickered in my mind once more. One might have thought, from the look on her face, that she had uttered God's own word. Even if she had, stubbornness would still forbid me from admitting it. I began to sort the mail on the table by category: bills, circulars that I would take home and recycle myself, and other. Ernestine's face spasmed for a moment: surprise, irritation, or gratitude? However she felt, I continued my sorting.

"And so I boarded the ship and went straight to my room. Rather small, yes, cramped and dark, but this was an adventure, and adventure often yields privation, which demands fortitude, which I have in abundance. The berth was truly no more than that, a small enclosed bed with scarcely enough room for my trunk. But it met my minimum needs, and what could I do but be grateful? Sleep beckoned, even in those unideal conditions, and I duly gave in. But the next day I awoke ready to take on my favorite role: voyeur!"

I snorted.

"Laugh all you want, Cloris. I have always been a great watcher of people, an outside observer, and relish what I learn from that purview. To board *The Voyeur* seemed almost too perfect, rather too suited to me, and the gentleman was right that what it offered was, simply, everything: everything you could ever want to see. Now, of course, much that comprises this 'everything' was simply shocking, disgusting, crude, and lewd. I did not wish to observe the act of copulation, nor did I wish to glimpse nude bodies writhing to the beat of an unfamiliar music."

"Ernestine, you boarded a cruise ship—pardon me, a starship—called *The Voyeur*. It sounds sleazy as hell to me. What would you expect but that sort of thing?" The mail before me lay in three piles. The vertiginous stack of circulars teetered on the verge of collapse. I divided that pile in two and folded my hands before me, awaiting a response.

She glared above her empty plate. I noticed that her housecoat had a yellow stain on its collar but did not dare point it out.

"Oh, Cloris," she began, settling into a familiar argumentative mode. "You're a real pill sometimes, you know that? Excuse me, but have you ever bothered exploring the galaxy around us? You'd find that lots of people elsewhere have minds quite a bit broader than yours—less inclined to sleaze. And you will have to take it on faith that there was much else there to draw the eye and mind for us voyeurs of nobler calling, a few of the carnal pleasures notwithstanding. If you don't want to listen, to give me your attention sans judgment—well, you can feel free to go home and return to your macramé. Or whatever it is you do to fill your time."

In silence we met each other's eyes. A long minute passed and then another. I stood up and walked to the sink, where water flowed weakly from a rust-stained faucet, and tried but failed to erase all trace of coffee from my mug. Back at the table, I sighed and waved my hand, prompting her to proceed.

"A zoo full of alien creatures—but you probably wouldn't care much about that. A library, granting access to the greatest volumes known to the galaxy. I couldn't help but slip a copy of my own book in there. Fortunately, I rarely leave home without a spare. I could go on, but there was one thing in particular that really drew me in—one thing I wanted to tell you about." Her voice quavered for a moment, and something in her manner shifted. It seemed that her muscles tensed; she grew defensive or wary. Then she cleared her throat and resumed.

"I spent all day wandering the ship, going in and out of the zoo and the library and the coffee shops and so on. And at the end of the day I wanted a meal, and maybe just a little drink to calm my nerves. So I asked around, and the word was that there was one bar you just couldn't miss. That's what they said. The name of this place was Scopophilia. It took me quite a while to find—way at the other end of the ship, the opposite end from the sleeping berths. It looked funny. The lighting was dark, but all the walls and the tables and chairs, everything, were in pastel colors. The pastel and dim lightning made it feel sort of eerie—haunted. It's been my experience that interior decoration on other planets is often disarming. Really, all judgments of taste—they differ so much from one species to another.

"Anyway, a young person led me to a high, round table near the back. I had to ask to be seated closer to the stage, and she complied but not without a look of disdain. Oh well. I had arrived just in time for the show, and I was not about to miss it because some gaggle of aliens in front of me were blocking my view. Onstage, a heavy black curtain made its squeaking way into a recess in the ceiling. No light shone; whoever stood there stood in shadow. But, soon, a thin trickling spotlight cast the performer's face in light, and I could see her pale and blue-toned skin, covered in garish makeup; her long flat limp blonde wig; her diaphanous garment, which might have been a sheet, cheaply sewn into a dress. If you could call it a dress. A voice resounded from somewhere behind me; the emcee said, 'And now, Helen of Troy, the Most Beautiful Woman in the World.'

"Now, that's a subjective judgment if ever I've heard one, not least because we spectators represented a good number of worlds, all of which, one might think, would have more to offer in the realm of beauty than this bedraggled performer. Nonetheless. We were there to enjoy the pleasure of looking, and I assumed that Helen of Troy, the Most Beautiful Woman in the World, not only offered a worthy prospect but enjoyed being looked at."

At this point, Ernestine's voice began to quaver. Her eyes roved around her kitchen and settled on her dog. Despite her apparent disapproval, despite her terse tone, it was clear that something that night had disturbed her.

"She sang. If you can call it singing. She sang a strange song that seemed a little familiar, though I could not recall having heard it. Something about how magic dances on a clock, how time is the magic length of God." I murmured "Buffy Sainte-Marie," but Ernestine ignored me, went on: "She didn't move at all, really, just barely swayed onstage in her terrible, booming voice. No: she *incanted*. She was reciting a spell on the unwilling masses. If you have not registered the fact, Cloris, she was a drag queen. And her voice pierced me like a needle, and it stung that badly. Oh my god. The thing is, Cloris, the thing is that I noticed, as she sang, that she looked remarkably like . . . She had blue skin—the slate-blue color of a corpse—and a terrible blond wig, but, when she moved in the spotlight, I saw it. She was the precise likeness, beneath false skin and hair, of him. Branson."

Ernestine, ever steely, looked suddenly so desperate. As though the cold night had come to claim her and found her bare—defenseless. As though the galactic paths she traveled had been totally evacuated. As though she had seen our brother.

My face must have been a mirror of hers. She said, "I had thought that he was . . ."

I nodded. My mouth felt dry. The room around us contracted, disappeared, and we floated alone with the remains of what we had thought to be unassailable truth.

My sister nodded. "And yet. There he was, I swear it. And doesn't that name just sound like him? 'Helen of Troy, the Most Beautiful Woman in the World.' The entire epithet, every time; no abbreviations. No compromises!

"Was beauty," Ernestine asked in a voice that was soft, shorn of its typical brash confidence, "our perception—we in the audience—or was it an essential quality of her being? She looked like a corpse; perhaps she was dead, and her body lived on in some other state we scarcely understand. She. Or he. Branson. I swear it was him. He was singing of the magic length of God and swaying, very gently, on his feet. And it was a very pretty thought to imagine that Helen of Troy, the Most Beautiful Woman in the World, was looking right at me as she swayed. But such a thought ended in conjunction with the song, and that is when she fled the stage; the lights went up; the show was declared, by that selfsame master of ceremonies, to be over. Helen of Troy, the Most Beautiful Woman in the World, had departed, and so had he."

Ernestine clasped her hands before her plate. She sat and said no more. Cheryl stirred behind us. And, after a very long spell of quiet, I said, "Ernestine."

"Yes, Cloris?"

"Is there more to the story?"

"There is not. The end has come. I retreated to my berth and slept all night. The next day, I found a trader whose little ship would depart that afternoon and bring me very close to Earth. I just got back this morning. Haven't even unpacked."

She stood and ambled to the sink, where she deposited plate and fork. From one pocket of her housecoat her hand drew out a purple leash, which she clipped to the collar around Cheryl's neck. After some exaggerated stretching, Cheryl followed her companion to the door. The thick sourness of dread suffused the air as I sat at the table, looking at the piles of my sister's mail. She and the dog left me alone with the faint sense that Branson could be here with us, except that I knew that to be impossible. An image surfaced that I would have preferred not to see: his face, his face, his face.

When at last Ernestine and Cheryl returned from their walk, neither of us spoke. Her face looked drawn, nearly corpselike. It seemed to me that her gaze was fixed on a point so distant it might have been that alien sun. For a

moment the image occurred to me—a flaming star that
sped our way and swallowed us whole, obliterating not
just us and the house that held us but the entire wretched
planet. And it occurred to me to speak it aloud and allow
it to sit there between us, though I did not indulge the
impulse.

Of course I did not believe her story. And after Ernestine gave Cheryl a treat and lumbered to her chair and
sat down once more, I felt moved to say so. Perhaps the
surge of perversity that then pulsed within me should
have encouraged me to pursue a line of inquiry or to
deny her stories outright, to insist that she was an invet-
erate liar and charlatan (which she was). But instead it
drove me to take a different tack.

Hands clasped, eyes sure, I looked at my sister and said,
"Ernestine, what really happened after you returned to
your booth? Why don't you tell me the end of the story?"

She gave one miserable shriek of a laugh. "I gave it to
you; you've got it!" Her face took on a bleak cast as she
sighed and lit a cigarette.

"Couldn't you have smoked that outside?"

She shook her head, a firm no. "If you want the end
of the story, dear sister, then why should I not oblige?
Once the show ended, we began to stand up. Some of us,
I presumed, would stay to chat and drink and do the other things that patrons do. But self-restraint is my watch-
word when I travel the galaxy, and no energy remained in
me for such leisurely pursuits. My little sleeping chamber
beckoned, and in that direction my feet swiftly took me.

The halls of *The Voyeur* are narrow and, at that time, they were dimly lit—evoking the night that did not exist for us, then near no sun. Rather, nothing but night existed. Anyway, scarcely any others traveled those corridors; for a time I had the feeling, stoked by the show at Scopophilia, of having slid into an empty world.

"As I left, I happened to spy the master of ceremonies shuffling away, in the same direction that I was taking. The temptation to follow him rose within me, but a more direct approach seemed wise. I sped up and soon overtook him.

"'Sir,'" I called, combating distaste at his tiny form, which resembled that of a pill-bug, though he stood as upright as I did. And he evidently possessed vocal cords of some sort or another. Or made use of a technology I could scarcely imagine, which permitted communication, as well as the deception of my senses. Would he—I dared wonder—roll away if frightened? He stopped and waited for me to speak. And I did: 'Where did Helen of Troy, the Most Beautiful Woman in the World, scamper off to? I would like to offer her my deepest and most profound respects.'"

"The pill-bug continued to stare. And I heard a voice, which to my ear now sounded distinctly robotic. He said, 'Oh. That's a hologram. We just use her for the shows. There's no real person.'"

"I said, 'A hologram? But surely she must be based on a real person—a simulacrum of the real, composed of light and strings of code, no?'"

"The pill-bug replied disappointingly: 'I don't know, lady. We've used her for years.' And then he turned and began to walk away, ignoring me as I called after him: 'But how could I find out?'

"I made my way to the berths. I entered mine and slept. And now. The end. The real end."

"That's all, Ernestine?" I asked. I felt ready to stand up and leave.

"That's all, sister. The genuine end. I am afraid, Cloris, that what I have given you is no more than a shaggy dog story. A tale to entice you—but one that has neither moral nor point. One whose mystery is perhaps irresolvable."

"Well, that's true. There was no reason to tell me any of this. To bring up all of this about—about Branson. Completely unnecessary." I rose and moved to retrieve my coat.

Ernestine had begun to mutter. Perhaps she meant me to hear, but the feeling struck me that I was eavesdropping, intruding on an intense and sudden privacy. She said, "Is it only when we believe ourselves most in control that we are most caught within time's trap? You see the shadow, the shadow, the beast within the shadow, the undying flame that burns at the heart of the darkest well in the world, and you think a way out is imminent, no? But delusion, utterly absolute, forms a hard and impenetrable shell around the sticky sorrow at the center of every single sorry life. I wonder whether she knew it, whether she understood the fundamental nature of our condition."

At that point she stopped, and she cleared her throat, and she lit another cigarette and looked my way.

"Do you understand it, Cloris?"

I sighed. "No," I said. My coat bedecked my shoulders. My bag was in my hand. The front door stood only a meter or so away, as the crow flies, though it suddenly seemed as distant as whatever desolate planet *The Voyeur* might now idly circle.

Ernestine cleared her throat and said, "I don't either. Not a whit. I'll call you after my next trip. I'm sure you'd be eager to hear all about it."

I smiled, made a gesture with my head that could have indicated yes or no or something altogether ambiguous—even I am not sure where my intentions lay and what it was I wanted her to see—and left her there alone at the table.

Seren's Day

~ David Bradley

As evening stars ignited, Dewin hunted, dripping and muddied, all the lawn dewy, raindrops falling from leaves as he went. The air was thick, the sky dank cotton wetted, all the world descending from day into night; brown'd light, brown'd mist, brown'd sight; water pooled and puddled; midge clouds and mosquito failed on the thick of his arms and the thick of his legs as he trod his way.

He felt all 'round him the spiorad asleeping as they nested, great taproots writhing about them, warm in their places, hollows and hovels, his spell invasive and slowly waking them. His music worked its way to them, whetted their appetites for such love and mystery as he swung to them. His web he spun about them, drawing them sticky and sweet from their drowse. In them they felt the pull of his spinning and his weaving and the lore of straw meadows and blighted harvests and a vow of granges overflowing with gold. And they wept all of them with hungor and drede, all of them but one.

The moment came, the moment Dewin'd foretold, the moment he'd created, the moment that the loose eyes of the feral fell upon him. Somewhere, there, awakened in the periphery, burrowing from hiding, the vines and the crawlers alive, tendrils reaching even deeper still, countless fingers stretched upward and outward from the wintwiges they'd weaved in their waiting, the fantoma felt of his coming and he, mighty Dewin, sensed of their waking. Onward still fair and infinite hedra moved about them, clawing blind through ancient peat, sweat sheets of silt laid by sruth when it was deep and far and wide, ten thousand lives of inundation and inferno and plague and plenty, one after another, lain atop each other and atop each other more, strangling in their cradle Lady's Mantle and spreading thick Foxglove, always; patient and planning and understanding, until the loam and the turf and the very earth itself had become fantoma and they, in turn, had become the very earth. And all their eyes fell upon Dewin, liquid eyes as salt as sea, ancient sea, eternal grandmother's grandfather's grandmother of Etang Bleu, home to all water, she most clear, she most pure, she most serene and chill'd to her icy heart.

Many were they wounded, broken wing and tongues twisted and torn and flayed, Dewin's curse'd damnation having drawn them in and taken them in and then thrown them aside. They lay in states of repose, nursing wounds both real and imagined, some few plotting their escape, some few daring horrible revenge, but more, and more than that, seeking only the dark and the damp and the warmth of their dug dens.

Fated that sweetest of days was Seren, hard of shell, long of gate and thrice eyed, to be drawn by the song of Man from her leafy bed of Vervain. Others withered, their vines bent and misshapen, and withdrawing for all of time. But Seren, weird queen of honey and heat, hidden in lengths of locks, depthless eyes pitch and fire, knew desire as an ocean rising.

On Dewin strode, confident one would follow, one each day, one whose hunger and ache t'would overcome, draw her out, draw her to him, out of the weeds and the stench and the mawing greenwood, moving beside the trail, not so silent as she dreamed, until the moment it seemed she would fail, and this day Seren was called. And she knew him before she saw him and he saw her before he knew her. The cord that bound them was knotted and noosed on the day of days, before even Seren was conceived in the fertile mud of lochan, before even Dewin was hatched in the first of fire, before even rocks were hurled from Hadean's sea. And it knotted them, him to her and her to he, she and his footsteps and he his ritual path, through pools of liquid clay, across the forest floor, their eyes rolling with their fear and their lust and their hunger.

The moon looked down as Seren followed, helpless and wanton to his magick, her trail slick and grease, through a maze of hedgerow battlements and hand hewn bawn. On Dewin's lawn the hives were settled for their slumber, beobread sweet wafted, and the lowing faded from the grange. Meat was hung and netted from slaughterhouse eaves, and baying wolves retreated as he came. Through his garden awash in Beelzebub's Wort and Poppy, Witch Hazel and Nightshade, his home overgrown by Orchid and Henbane, all staggered at Seren's fatal honey'd breath.

Flame gasped in Dewin's grate, dying eyes glowed their last in coal spent, twigs and kindling ash white, wisps of smoke dwindling to the rafters and on into the blackish night. On the hob heated blade and bowl, Dewin's repast, hare and root, thick and fatty, set aside to break his fast come morning light. Dewin's ritual unchanged.

Seren traced the earthen walls, blood pulse and sweat-ed brow, her sapphire eye following Dewin as he led her, and her sapphire eye following Dewin as he turned to her, and her sapphire eye following Dewin as he approached, hard and determined and knowing; Dewin's ritual unchanged.

Seren took her breath and spread herself and braced herself, her sapphire eye following Dewin's steps fast toward her, her sapphire eye following Dewin's lust for her, her sapphire eye following Dewin's eyes upon her; Dewin's ritual unchanged.

Seren hissed and raised her hood, drawing Dewin to her, wrapping herself around him, holding herself to him, closer and closer still, stretching her arm to her arm and her leg to her leg, gripping herself to herself, pulling herself to herself. And Dewin was lost within her, knowing not what was become, until lungful breath escaped him, and bones brittle became. Sweet Serin's teeth, as sharpened blade, were bared and sank, poisoned and painless and deep, into Dewin's bared flesh.

There was a being, the soul of the Man, perched on a particle deep in darkest Dewin, that recognized the moment, the moment of moments, and watched as if from afar, yet within and without it, the crushing of the meat and the splintering of the bone and the piercing of the heart. The light turned blacker still, and cried and called out to eternity as it was extinguished. And then mighty Dewin was no more.

All through the night Serin slumbered and fed, and wept and bled, her lust and love ingested and dead, until the dawn, nursed life unto the fire and built of Dewin a vast and glowing pyre.

And then it was the day, and the keep knew of green shoots and scarlet fruit. And Seren saw it, and named it, and knew it well. For that was the morn of Seren's day.

Marnie and Kyle in the Quick 'n' Now

~ Jason Washer

Eleven-thirty PM and it's freezing rain outside. I've already swept the store and emptied the trash, and haven't seen a single customer since our shift started. I can't see past the gas pumps and the darkness to the street beyond, but I know it's deserted, too slick to travel. The roads were treacherous on the way in and I should have stayed home.

Kyle's been stocking the beer freezer for what seems like hours. Through the freezer door I watch him sit down onto a case of beer and hunch forward over his phone. He stays like that for a while, his fingers occasionally flicking at the screen, and I don't want to know what he's looking at. I pull a half dozen magazines from the rack and bring them back up to my perch at the register and start flipping through them. Later I'm turning the last page on the last magazine and digging through my purse for nail polish when I hear the squeal of the freezer door opening and see Kyle hugging himself as he walks up to the register. His cheeks are blue.

"You were in there a long time," I say, glancing up at the clock behind the register. Hardly any time has passed at all, but I don't retract or apologize. Instead I lean into it, "I hope it was good for the phone too . . ."

"Don't be a perv, Marnie," Kyle says, not meeting my eye, and then I really don't want to know what he was looking at on his phone. It takes a minute but he eventually blushes and tells me to fuck off, but not with any particular vehemence, only a mild shame. Tonight's my third shift at the Quick 'n' Now, just two nights past my orientation shift with Jamie, and only my first working with Kyle. He's as awkward as he sounds, and always was, even back in school. He sits next to me behind the counter, the two of us up on stools, silently surveying the store, waiting for someone to come in.

No one does.

"Did you sweep?" he asks, like he's my supervisor. He's not. It's my third day but it's only his second month.

"Yup," I say, and then because I can I ask, "Did you stock the cooler while you were in there?"

"Yup," Kyle says, and then glances down at the empty trash bin behind the register. "Did you empty the trash?"

I glance from the empty can to Kyle and try to hold his eye for a moment so he knows just how stupid of a question that was but he quickly looks away. Someone needs to come into the store soon and buy something or I'll lose my mind. I'm certain if this quiet and boredom continues for another seven hours Jamie will find us in the morning at each other's throats like feral dogs, one of us wearing the other's blood as war paint. Or worse yet making out in the cooler.

"How's your mom?" I finally ask, reduced to small talk. He looks at me, an eyebrow raised, confused. I don't know his mom, and hardly know him, other than for the years we passed each other silently in the halls of Ripley's schools. A dozen years of school for a job at the Quick n' Now, and Jamie had me trained in less than an hour: here's the registers, card everyone under forty for beer, and don't forget to sweep and take out the trash. We spent the rest of the shift chatting, and then had beers in his car up by the airport. I'll admit it, Jamie's pretty hot.

"Dead," Kyle says with something like glee. Not glee that his mom is dead, but glee that I asked such a stupid question. Of course she was dead, and had been since sixth grade. Everyone in town knew his mom was dead, even me. She drove into a lake.

"Sorry," I say, and I mean it. I should have remembered. It was a big deal back then, and the only thing anyone in school or town talked about, and then everything went back to the way it was. At least for us. "I forgot."

"It's okay," he says, still not meeting my eyes. When he says it it comes out mumbled, and sounds like 's'kay' and then for some dumb reason I feel even worse, because I remember that I never told him I was sorry when his mom died in sixth grade; and no, I didn't just remember. I knew and I've known that I never did. Even at the start of the shift, I knew. I could feel it between us even if I didn't know at first what it was. I'm not sure if anyone at school ever told him they were sorry about his mom.

"The floor . . ." Kyle says, this time meeting my eye for a moment before looking away again.

"I told you I swept," I say, sharper than I should have. His mom died after all, and for me anyways it's as fresh as if it just happened, though I guess he's been living with it, or without her, so he's probably used to it by now. Could a person get used to their mom driving into a lake?

"No," Kyle says, getting up from his stool and walking around to the other side of the counter. He points to the cooler, "the floor. In the cooler. It's cracked."

I follow him into the cooler so he can show me his discovery and I hope he doesn't think this is the part where we make out, because it isn't. The door seals behind us and it's freezing in the small and brightly lit beer cooler. Neither of us is wearing a jacket. I hug myself for warmth and he points to the floor, and sure enough, there's a crack in the tile.

"It's new," he says, crouching down on his heels. He runs his fingertips lightly up and down the thin foot long crack in the floor. "It wasn't there yesterday..."

"Someone must have dropped a case of beer," I say. "Better call the cops."

He squints down at the crack, "Do you see it?"

"What?" All I see is the cracked tile, and Kyle, shivering on his knees in the cooler. It's freezing in here, and I'm freezing too. Fuck this, "I'm going back to the register."

"The reflection in the crack," Kyle leans down, his face inches from the floor. "Or maybe it's a light?"

"I don't see it, and I'm cold," I move toward the freezer door.

"Just look at it," he motions for me to come closer. "Come look. Don't you see it?"

"No, and if you think I'm getting down on the floor with you—"

"Marnie, please."

"Fine," I say, and kneel down beside him to stare at the cracked tile. There's a reflection, he's right. Or maybe it's a light. "So someone left the basement lights on. Big deal."

We're both kneeling on the cold tile, our faces pressed close to the floor staring at the crack and he looks up at me, his face inches from mine.

"Nope," I say, clambering to my feet. "Not tonight. Not going to happen."

He looks up at me, confused for a moment, until his face registers understanding. "Stop being a perv. And don't you get it?"

"What?"

"There's no basement."

Back at the register I glance up at the clock and it's still barely half past eleven. Time is crawling by, and this is officially the longest shift ever. Outside the sleet continued, and the constant pattering of the freezing rain on the roof rang on. I watch Kyle staring down at the slowly rotating hotdogs for what seems like minutes, until I can't stand it anymore.

"Jamie never told me," I say, and Kyle looks up at me, his spell broken. "About the hotdogs? Do they ever get swapped out? Or are those the same ones from the grand opening?"

Kyle shook his head no, and smiled. "I've never seen them changed since I've been here. And I've never sold one. Maybe on the day shift?" He grabbed the tongs. "Want one?"

"God no," I say, "You go ahead."

Kyle sets the tongs down, "Nah, not hungry. Maybe later."

He hops back up onto the stool next to me and we sit silently for what seems like hours. Finally I'm unable to stand it any longer, the awkwardness too thick, and I break the spell and blurt out, "Jamie seems nice."

Kyle snorts, a grin on his face. "Everyone thinks so."

"Don't you?"

"He's a great manager. Really nice," he says, and I see the expression on his face and hear the bitter longing in his voice and realize that I'm not the only one who's been drinking beers up by the airport with Jamie. The manager of the Quick n' Now is an equal opportunity employer.

"So nice," I agree softly, and stare hopefully at the door, willing someone to come in. No one does. This might be the longest night of my life. "Is it always this slow?"

"Maybe it's a crawl space?" Kyle asks, staring over at the beer cooler again. "For the pipes?"

"Maybe," I say, and then add. "It's probably just a reflection."

"An optical illusion," Kyle says. "The way the lights are hitting it."

"A delusion."

"What?" Kyle asks me.

"My dad, he always says 'optical delusion.'"

"Yeah," Kyle says, and then gets up from the stool. He goes into the office and comes out with his jacket in one hand and a screwdriver in the other. "I'm just going to take another look."

I watch the freezer door close behind him, and I sit under the store's buzzing fluorescent lights and wait. After a while I get up and grab another handful of magazines to skim through even though I've read them all before. He's gone for what seems like a really long time, though the clock is still showing barely half past eleven when he comes back out of the freezer with the screwdriver in his hand. He nods at me as he walks past the register and into Jamie's office. I can hear the drawers of the file cabinet banging open and shut, and when he walks back into the cooler he's carrying a hammer in addition to the screwdriver.

I wait at the register for what feels like an hour and then grab my jacket and follow him into the cooler.

Kyle's on the floor wailing away at the tile with the hammer. The walk-in cooler is filled with a haze of dust, and tiny chips of tile are flying through the air and pinging off the cases of beer. The hairline crack is now a hole big enough to reach an arm into. A faint yellow light streams up from the opening.

"Holy shit," I say over the sound of the smashing tile. Kyle's arm is robotically swinging the hammer at the floor, over and over and over again, the hole getting bigger and bigger until it's almost two feet across. "Jamie's going to kill you."

Kyle stops swinging the hammer and looks up at me questioningly, and then says, "It's not so bad, I just wanted to see . . ." He looks down at the ruined floor, realizing what he's done. "Oh shit."

"Yeah," I say. "You're fucked."

"I didn't think I . . . I wasn't thinking. I didn't realize."

"You were in here for a long time," I say. "How could you not realize?"

He pulls out his phone and glances at the clock, and shakes his head, "No, I wasn't."

"Yeah, you were. You're really fucked." I kneel down beside him and peer into the hole. It drops six feet down to another ceramic tiled floor, and a hallway that veers off to the side. The light is coming from off to the side, further in. "What is this?"

Kyle shrugs and wipes sweat from his pocked forehead with the sleeve of his jacket. "An unfinished basement. Utility room, maybe."

"With no stairs?" I say, thoroughly creeped out. I shiver, maybe from the cold. I'm pretty sure that Kyle has stumbled into someone's murder hole, and that there's probably a dozen body's stacked like cordwood just out of sight around the corner.

"And no door," Kyle says, and then, "There has to be a door."

"Where?"

Kyle shrugs again, "There has to be."

I stand up and say "Nope. That's enough. Fuck this. We'll sweep all this shit down into the hole and just tell Jamie we dropped a keg on the floor."

"You think he'll believe it?"

"Sure. And it doesn't matter if he doesn't. I'm going to get the broom out of the office."

I grab the broom out of the office and glance at the clock as I head back into the cooler to see how many more hours of this I have left. 11:30. It has to be broken, or the clock's batteries are dead, so I pull out my own phone to check the time and my battery's dead too. Awesome.

"Kyle," I say as I'm pulling open the cooler door. "What time is it?" He's not in the cooler. "Kyle?"

"Down here," He pokes his head up through the hole in the floor.

"What the hell!" I jump back, startled, and may have peed a little bit. "You scared me. What are you doing?"

"I just wanted to see where the light was coming from," Kyle says, ducking his head back down into the hole.

"And?" I crouch down near the hole just in time to see him duck around the corner and out of sight. "Kyle?"

"Just a corridor going down, and then it turns off to the right again."

"Come back out," I say, and I can hear his feet scuffing away. "Right now. You shouldn't be down there."

His voice echos up to me, "I'm just going to look. I'll be right out."

"Jamie's going to kill you," I say, and then regret it.

"It's fine," he calls. "I just want to look. Be right back."

"Kyle," I say as I listen to his footsteps get further and further away.

I stare at the hole in the cooler floor and I wait.

I pull out my phone again to check the time before I remember my battery's dead, and then I walk back out into the store and pull a charger off the shelf next to the Tylenol and tampons. I rip open the charger and then try to plug my phone in behind the register but of course it's the wrong size phone plug. Of course it is.

I look up at the broken clock and try to work backwards to figure out when Jamie will come in and our shift will be over, and I think about the magazines and the sweeping and Kyle breaking open the floor with the screwdriver and the hammer and I don't know. It has to be four a.m. by now, or later. It feels later. It's been such a long shift. When Jamie gets here in the morning I'm going to quit. I go back into the cooler and sit down on a case of beer to wait for Kyle to come back. I try not to imagine Jamie wearing his skin.

I stare at the hole and wait and before long I can't even feel my hands anymore and my ass is numb from sitting for so long. My nose runs from the cold, the sleeve of my jacket damp with snot. Occasionally I give a halfhearted yell down into the hole for Kyle, but he never answers and after a while my voice goes hoarse and my throat grows sore from shouting.

I try counting to measure the passage of time, but invariably my mind wanders and I forget where I am in the count and have to start over. I consider leaving my vigil at the hole more than once, but I don't. Where would I go? And once I stop expecting the shift to end, or anyone to come into the store, the waiting grows less painful.

I think about Kyle's mom a lot. Was there a point in the lake as the water rushed up around the car that she changed her mind and said fuck this? A moment where she fought back? And if she did change her mind how hard and how long did she try to get out of that car? At some point did she just give up and accept the water rushing in and over her?

I yell for Kyle again, loud, and this time when he doesn't respond I drop down into the hole.

I walk for longer than I can remember. The passage slowly descends, each long and tiled hallway eventually turning right into another and then another, and in this way I slowly descend until I almost forget where I'm going or what I'm looking for. Hours or years later, I don't know anymore, I turn right for must be the thousandth time and the hallway terminates in a dimly lit and low ceilinged alcove no bigger than the beer cooler.

Kyle and Jamie are sitting at a card table and Kyle's laughing like he just heard the world's best joke. Jamie can be wickedly funny, especially when he has you alone in a car by the airport, or in a small room deep underground.

"Hey guys," I interrupt, a little worried that I'm ruining Jamie's joke.

"Hi Marnie," Kyle says, holding up a hand in greeting.

"Want a beer, Marnie?" Jamie grins and holds up a sweaty can of Pabst. I love his smile, I can't help myself, and almost take the beer, but instead I shake my head no and offer him a tight smile in return.

"I'm not thirsty," I tell Jamie, and I notice Kyle's not drinking either. I turn to Kyle, "I was waiting for you. You didn't come back."

"Sorry," Kyle says. "We were just hanging out. I lost track of time."

"Let's go back up to the store now, Kyle," I say, and instead of answering me Kyle just looks at Jamie, waiting for him to answer. "Our shift is almost over."

Jamie smiles that smile he has, all charm and promise, and he looks at me like I'm the only person left in the world, like it's just me and him alone at the end of the world, as if Kyle's not even here, and then he shoves out a metal folding chair from the table with a small booted foot and says, "Sit and have a beer, Marnie. Let's hang out for a while."

"I'd love to, but we left the story empty," I say, and then add, "Sorry."

"No worries," Jamie says after he downs the last of his Pabst and crushes the can. He tosses the can onto the floor near my feet, and then he's somehow popping the tab on another can. "It's fine, really. The store can take care of itself. Kyle, tell her to sit down."

"Sit down Marnie," Kyle says, not meeting my eye. "Jamie was telling a story."

I smile politely, but I don't sit. I know I can't sit if I want to leave, and I really, really want to leave, even if the beer is starting to look good now. I didn't think I was thirsty, but maybe I am. I'm also very cold. I tell Kyle, "We should go now."

Kyle looks from me to Jamie, hoping for his permission. It doesn't come. Jamie just smiles that smile of his like this is all perfectly normal. Nothing's wrong, and why would anyone ever want to leave?

"Kyle," I say, and he smiles apologetically, and this time meets my eye, but doesn't move. Maybe he can't move, I don't know. I turn to Jamie, and try not to think about what we did together in the backseat of his car, because he doesn't look quite the same anymore; he seems older now, thinner, his hair greasier than before, his bones prominent. He's wearing a thin pair of blue jeans with the cuffs tucked into the brown boots, and a buttoned up shirt that I swear is straight out of the seventies, and not retro fashion or seventies inspired, but an actual and threadbare shirt pulled from the seventies. I realize that he's very old, older than even the nineteen seventies. "Jamie," I say to him, trying to smile, trying to not let on that I know how old he is, "we've got to get back to the store. Our shift is almost over . . ."

"Nah," Jamie says, and he's not smiling anymore, and maybe he never was. "Stop me if you've heard this one."

"We have to leave," I say again.

"I know you've heard it before," he says to Kyle, and he winks, his eyelid slowly folding shut like a bat's wing before reopening. His hand rests intimately on Kyle's shoulder, his fingernails long and dirty, brown with decades of stain.

"Jamie, please," I say, and I realize that he won't willingly let us go. He can't.

"There was a boy, we'll call him Kyle," Jamie laughs. "And his mom drove into a lake."

"Don't be an ass, Jamie," I say. "I know the story. We're leaving now."

"No. And you don't know the whole story—"

"Kyle," I say. "Get up. We're leaving now."

"Marnie?" Kyle says, half up from his chair, and his eyes are boring into mine, pleading with me, hoping.

Fuck this. Fuck Jamie. Fuck the store. Fuck all of it. I reach over the card table and grab Kyle's arm and try to pull him the rest of the way to his feet. His arm is cold, freezing, and Kyle is shivering, his face pale, his lips blue.

"We're going," I tell Jamie as I pull Kyle up from the chair. Kyle looks at me, his eyes still pleading with me, and I'm remembering back to middle school after his mom died and I really, really wish I had told him how sorry I was. It was a really shitty deal for him, and I should have said something, should have said anything, but I didn't.

We stumble past Jamie and he doesn't look anything like Jamie from the car anymore, not even close, not even human, and then Kyle and I are out of the alcove and we're back in the narrow corridor.

"I'm so sorry," I say to Kyle. I can hear him just behind me, following me, shivering, his breath coming in frozen hitches as we climb the long hallway back up to the beer cooler. "I really am. I should have said something."

"It's okay, really."

"No, it's not. Kids are assholes. I was an asshole."

"Marnie, let it go, okay. It was a long time ago," Kyle tells me, but it really wasn't. Six years, a couple of thousand days. I couldn't imagine how he could let it go so soon. "I've moved past it, and you should too."

"How can you move past it?" I ask incredulously, trudging back up the long halls toward the surface. I listen to Kyle's feet scuffing the tile behind me, but I don't hear anyone behind Kyle. Not yet. I wish I could remember how far away the store was. "I don't believe you."

"She did the best she could," Kyle says.

"Bullshit," I answer, "absolutely fucking bullshit. She was a bitch and should have done a lot better by you," and when he doesn't reply I realize I've gone too far. Awesome. First I ignore him when his mom dies, like he wasn't even there, pretending like nothing ever happened, and then I call his dead mother a bitch. Nice going. "Sorry."

He still doesn't answer, and we keep walking. Time passes, and we must be close to the store by now, but I have no way to know with my phone's dead battery. I spend most of the walk wondering if Jamie's coming after us, and if he is what he'll do when he catches us. I'm tired. After a while I realize that he can't follow us. He's too old, too set in his ways by a thousand years of time and death washing over him. He can't move, and he doesn't want to move. He never moved, even in the car by the airport; he was just a daydream, a passing fancy, a wish sworn and quickly recanted.

He just waits.

Kyle and I are safe, for now.

"Kyle?"

He doesn't answer me, and hasn't for the last hours and miles, though I still hear him behind me.

"I said that I was sorry," still no answer. "I'm sure she did her best."

My mind wanders back to the sixth grade, and Kyle, and his absence. I hadn't told him I was sorry about his mom driving into the lake. Not then and not ever. How could I?

"Kyle, don't be a dick. Answer me. Say something." And then even though I know I shouldn't, I turn to look at him, and then he's gone, vanished from the long tiled hall.

He's been gone for a long time, forever twelve years old.

A woman who drives into a lake, that's tragic, I remember my dad saying. Who knows what demons that poor woman might have been facing? But a woman who drives into that same lake with her twelve year old son in the back seat? Then she's not a woman facing demons anymore, is she? That's too generous of an assessment. She is the demon.

A minute or a lifetime later I finally see the fluorescent lights of the beer cooler. I climb up through the hole and stagger out into the Quick n' Now. The clock is still stuck at eleven-thirty. It's still sleeting out, still dark. No one has come in all this time.

"Kyle?" I call softly to the empty store, and I know he won't answer. I'm alone. I grab the same magazines I've read a dozen times before from the rack and bring them up to the register and start flipping through them. Nothing has changed. The fluorescent lights buzz overhead, the sleet rattles on the roof, and I wait.

Hand of Glory

~ Roni Stinger

I draw Fred's hand along my body, following the curve of my hipbone, the contour of my belly, tracing the lines of long faded stretch marks with his fingers. My breath hitches, a mix of desire and guilt. I dig my heels into the satin sheets. Lavender essence fills the bedroom with a slight undertone of salt and vinegar. Our love is now forbidden.

He always made me cum first . . . and last. I'd had a few boys before him. They never cared much what I liked. Never taking the time to satisfy me. They took what they wanted and left me to pleasure myself without them. Not that I minded getting myself off, but it wasn't quite the same as sharing it with another.

Fred was different. He enjoyed making me cum. His cock growing so hard as waves of orgasms rushed through my body while he expertly moved his fingers on my clit, slow circles the way I liked, dipping his free fingers into my pussy. God. Just thinking about him made me hot.

☉

His hand is large with thick fingers, calloused from years of labor, but it moves across my body gently. Smooth, thick skin with a touch of dampness lights my nerve endings, leading the way into my pink silk panties. I roll my head back and close my eyes.

He always had a strong work ethic, joining his dad at the lumber mill as soon as he turned eighteen, supporting me and our baby when she arrived right after we both graduated high school. Baby Missy had my dark hair and his blue eyes. His curls and my dimples.

No one thought our marriage would last. We were both so young. Doomed to fail, as parents, as partners. Yet ten years on, our little girl played basketball in the driveway with her dad. He taught her to shoot and dribble. I taught her to bake, garden, and fish.

He and I had our fights. Marriage and parenting weren't easy, but make up sex was the best. We'd find a sitter and steal away, have sex in our car like teenagers.

His hand moves further into my panties, fingers cool, caressing the folds of my labia. My lips moisten in anticipation. I relax into the pillow. His musky tang envelops me.

☉

The other women shocked me, but I tried to understand. I'd had my own temptations but managed to resist. If I were truly honest, I had my own regrets. Times I would have given in had the opportunity arose. Things I wished I'd tried with one or more of my close friends.

It was long ago, and we'd both been so very young. Beneath the surface of any relationship, nothing's as easy as it appears. The many years I tried to understand his secrets and lies were eclipsed by the image of his hands caressing another, working their magic on someone else. That image haunted me through my forgiveness. My stomach grew sick each time I imagined his hands on another. I struggled to push those thoughts away.

I tried not to be selfish. Maybe. there was enough pleasure and love to go around. That's what my polyamorous friends had said. I almost believed, but his hands were mine, meant for only me.

His hand, warmed by the heat of my body, now belongs to only me, working the magic it knows so well. His fingers tease their entrance. Dripping and wanting, I beg and plead. Enter me.

On our twentieth anniversary, Missy went off to college. We were a couple again, instead of just a family. The house echoed with a silence that only my weeping filled. Fred's caresses brought comfort.

We went to restaurants we'd never been. Planned weekend getaways we'd dreamed of in our youth. We found each other and ourselves again.

I took up painting. Missy's old bedroom became my studio. Fred discovered woodworking. Our garage became his shop. In our bed, I found my voice again. No longer a reason to keep quiet with nobody else in the house. Our moans and my screams filled the rooms as we christened each one with our lovemaking. We were more turned on by each other than we'd ever been, playing new games and buying new toys. Falling deeper in love each day.

I thrust my hips upwards, panting as his fingers enter. They dive deep inside, first one . . . then two . . .then three. Every touch a stroke of erogenous tissue. Almost more than I can take. Almost.

Thirty years after our wedding, we'd beat the odds, made it through the disagreements, the fights, and the transgressions. Fred's hands caressed my arm to ease my nerves, held my waist when I needed comfort.

Missy made us grandparents of a sweet cherubic boy named Danny. He had her dark curly hair and his daddy's smile. Fred played peekaboo and pat-a-cake. Games he'd been too busy for when Missy was a baby.

I baked cookies like any good grandma. I worried so about that little one. What would his future be in this world I barely recognized? Fred's strong hands on my shoulders told me everything would be okay.

When we sent little Danny home, Fred and I made up for lost time together. Our love life had slowed, but his hands hadn't forgotten how to please. He took his time with my pleasure, and I took mine with his.

His hand, inside me. His thumb on my clit. The joints grown stiff but still workable. I guide them to my climax. My moans and screams fill the emptiness of our bedroom.

Fred was working on a new bathroom cabinet for Missy. She took pride in showing her friends the things her dad made.

I painted in my studio, a portrait of Fred and me inspired by a picture taken shortly after we'd met. I'd lost track of time. Fred always came in for a kiss before taking his evening shower. Then I'd clean up my project, and we'd spend the rest of the evening reading or watching old sitcoms we both enjoyed.

When the sun set behind the mountains and my studio dimmed beyond my ability to see, I went to the shop. He should have been in an hour ago.

The roar of the saw greeted me as I opened the door to the garage. At first, I couldn't figure out what I was seeing. Red fabric strewn across the floor. Fred hunched over the saw . . . no. The saw cut through him, still spinning as it protruded from his back. The red wasn't fabric. Blood and flesh flung from Fred's torso and splattered across the floor as he'd collapsed atop the blade. Piles of sawdust and blood indistinguishable from flesh and guts. I'd warned him against using the saw without its guard, but he said he'd be careful.

I stood gaping for what seemed a lifetime, but must have been seconds, before crossing the room and unplugging the saw. But it was much too late. It had been much too late, long before I entered the garage.

Nothing anyone could do, and I knew it. His flesh had gone ivory and scarlet. The blood drying to a crusty brown. I sunk to the concrete floor, cold traveling through my body. I wept for hours before forcing myself to get up and make that call. It was just Fred and me in the garage, adorned with his body parts.

I closed my eyes. It was almost as if nothing had happened, as if we were still happily together. When I opened them, on the floor only a few feet from where I sat, his right hand had fallen free of the mess that had once been my love.

His hand lay palm up, fingers curled like a dead spider's legs, waiting for someone to sweep the critter up. Inching forward, I picked up his hand and cradled it, hugging my love to my chest. The flesh was cool, but still his. The blood congealed at the ragged stump. Not a mar on the rest of the hand.

⊙

Holding his hand against my cheek, his fingers open and caress my skin, warm from my hot pussy. I close my eyes and drift.

I washed his hand in the sink and took it to my bedroom, placing it under the covers. Then I made the phone call. The paramedics arrived and called the morgue. The body bag resembled laundry more than something that was once human. No one asked questions, only offered condolences.

Fred came to me that night and whispered in my ear, his hand resting with me beneath the covers, laid on my waist, fingers reaching for the spots that he knew best.

When I close my eyes, he's still here, whispering in my ear. I guide his hand down, his fingers caress my clit, ready for our second round. When we finish, I'll set him back in the jar on the nightstand, preserving our love for another night.

Our years together aren't over yet.

KNIGHT of SWORDS .

Cans of Laugher, Jars of Tears

~ *J. P. Oakes*

Detective Ansible presses two fingers to the bridge of her nose and tries to will her headache away. "And we're absolutely sure that this guy was dead when he showed up for work this morning?"

The ME pokes in the chest cavity with a ballpoint pen. "Time of death is probably two days ago."

Ansible releases a sigh that is almost a moan. "God-damn East Theoran bullshit."

Two bodies lie on a hotel-room floor. CSU techs bustle around them. Out in the hall, West Theoran security forces swarm like wasps.

"You know what I would give," Ansible asks the ME, "for this to just be another dumb zombie case?"

The corpse by the ME's feet—until recently a bellhop—is a body become a cavity. The chest has been opened, ribs splayed, reaching imploringly for the heavens. Inside: no lungs, no heart, no liver, arteries, or veins. A space as dry and empty as a butcher's carcass.

The ME straightens, points her ballpoint at the second corpse. It's painted with a filthy palette of bruises, but it has all its organs at least.

"You know who that is, right?"

Ansible wishes she didn't. Wishes it wasn't Konstantin Böhm, part of the delegation come to this hotel to negotiate with the East Theorans; wasn't the main voice of dissension to the trade deal being organized. Wishes that if he was going to get murdered, he could have at least waited until her shift was over to do it.

"A moment detective?" one of the CSU techs calls to her. He's by the door with a brush and jar of black powder. His look doesn't telegraph good news.

"No useable prints?" she asks.

He sucks his teeth and steps aside to reveal the door.

It is like a monochromatic finger painting by a class of deranged toddlers. Fingerprints overlay each other on the door, the wall, the mirror. A veritable trail of them.

Ansible's headache intensifies.

After the Hierophantic Wars, the surviving factions fought over Theora like it was the last pie on the dinner table. As Ansible understands it, the only solution they could agree on was the worst one: slicing the city down the middle; splitting it into East and West. East Theora would belong to the Selazzi Regime, while West Theora would remain under Empirical control.

Border disputes had been constant since then. East Theoran agents—and other more outré things—are forever slipping into the West, and conversely, the West sends its own spies East, although from what Ansible

has heard, even with modern technology the number returning sane enough to have useful information is still
below ten percent.

And yet, despite all the bad blood, and the history, and
the vigorous, violent differences of opinion, the diplomatic
process has picked up momentum. And now a trade delegation is visiting from East Theora.

Except now, despite the eyes of the world on this microcosm, and despite all the security, the man who led those
railing against the deal is dead, and Ansible is left holding
the bag.

Ansible follows a trail of radial loops, tented arches, and
plain whorls plastered on walls, stair railings, and doors.
She drags two security guards after her, and chides at the
CSU tech as he paints his dust on the prints, trying to
follow them across patches of carpet and rug for empty,
tantalizing yards, before they reappear on an oak door,
an elevator panel.

Two floors down from the murder scene, they enter a
service corridor, and find a hallway become an abbatoir.
Organs are spread across the floor—greasy intestines; a
glistening liver; two lungs spread like sagging wings. A
maid stands at the corridor's far end, facing the corner,
shrieking.

The two guards turn ashen-faced. One bends over
breathing deeply. Ansible pushes through the gore, past
the heaving guards. As she reaches the corridor's far door,

she flashes a glance at the screaming nurse. She's halfway through the door before she registers what she saw: fingers protruding from the maid's screaming mouth, tucking away behind her teeth.

Ansible scrambles to bring her gun to bear, screams, "Freeze!"

The maid backhands her, sends her sliding through gore. Ansible tries to pick herself up, limbs responding distantly, and then the world above her detonates. Behind her, a guard's rifle blares a wild, fully-automatic burst of fire. The maid reels through the far doorway as the rounds strike her.

The gun runs dry. Anisible leaps up, scrambling gorily after the fallen body.

She's not fast enough.

When she punches through the door, the maid is bucking on the floor. Then she erupts like a piñata, ribs flying like candy.

Something bursts out of her. A ball of hands—some white, some black, some spattered with freckles, others knotted with arthritis. Some nails are blunt, others chewed, others manicured to sharp points. The creation— roughly the size of the beach ball she once tossed back and forth with her father on a childhood vacation—is too densely packed with digits for her to see how the palms join together.

It scrambles wildly down the hall, fingers dragging it along at madcap speed. Ansible fires, can't tell if she hits it or not, gives chase.

There's a stairwell ahead. It plunges down, sliding from railing to railing, barely controlled. She crashes after it, hearing the guards clattering after her. But by the time she reaches the bottom of the stairs, it's long gone.

She doubles over, panting, horrified.

Goddamn East Theoran bullshit.

The East Theorans aren't keen on her questioning their ambassador. She doesn't give them a choice.

They meet in a conference room attempting grandeur and failing. He's smaller than she expects, narrow and red-headed, wearing a sharply tailored pin-stripe suit. His face is a blizzard of scars, lines of white puckered flesh intersecting like webbing. Both his ears have been removed. He sits in a chair opposite her. Behind him hulks his bodyguard, looking somehow pieced together, as if not all of his body is organic to him. Next to him sits his translator, a young man dressed as if for a funeral, a slight plastic sheen to his skin.

"We've had an incident," Ansible says as she sits, then lays it out for him—the bodies, the chase, the creature. He doesn't blink. "Anything you want to say?"

For a long moment, she thinks he's just going to sit there staring through her. Then he lets out a long, shuddering hiss, slowly building in pitch until she thinks he's about to scream. Then it cuts off. "It reaches," he says in a voice painfully dry. "It grasps." The he reaches out toward her with a closed fist and pulls a heart out of nowhere.

He tucks the bloody organ into a pocket inside his suit.

The translator leans forward. "The creature you encountered," he says, "is known as a Manus Dei. It is a summoning, brought here by a practitioner. It is used to take possession of a host and enslave it to the practitioner's will."

Ansible waits for more. It doesn't come. "The practitioner's name ?"

The heart in the ambassador's pocket is staining his shirt red. He spits something thick and black onto the floor, scratches at it with his shoe.

"The ambassador is committed to the peace process," the translator says. "He believes trade agreements are the first step to a more open and trusting relationship. He is as horrified by this murder as you are and swears he has no idea who would act against him."

"Against him?" Ansible loses the struggle to suppress her incredulity. "The main opponent to his deal was just killed."

The ambassador leans forward, smiles. All his teeth, she sees, have been filed to points. "Through night I wander while around me birds flaps with wings like dark silk borne of worms grubbing through leaves infested with a mushroom that claws like a tower toward the heavens."

The translator runs a hand through his hair. "This deal is delicate," he says. "How does someone painting the East Theorans as murderers help us?"

☉

Later, Ansible sits in a makeshift incident room with a member of Empiricist foreign office, an emaciated-looking woman called Jennings.

"You think the East Theorans put some of it on?" she asks. "I mean, how would we know if they're just hamming it up for us?"

Jennings shakes her head. "I was part of a delegation sent there once. It gets-" She shudders. "-so much worse."

Unsettled, Ansible changes tack. "Is the murder of the ambassador's main opponent really bad for him?"

Jennings huffs mirthless laughter. "You hear that?" she says.

Ansible does. Böhm's supporterss flood the streets outside, their screams and protests breaking against the hotel's thick walls like surf.

"Does that," Jennings says, "sound like good news for this deal?"

"But the talks are still going on, right?"

Jennings chews her lip. "For now."

"So, what's riding on this deal?"

Jennings's attempt at a smile is horrific. "The specifics of the legislation aren't as important as the two sides just working together, coming up with some consistent rules, working on common problems, moving away from being opponents and toward being partners."

"But the specifics?" Murders, Ansible knows, rarely happen because people look at the big picture.

Jennings shrugs. "Updating tariffs means there are some winners, sure. Losers too."

"I'll want a list of those losers."

Jennings calls people. Ansible writes names on a chalk board. Goes back to one that Jennings paused over.

"Pierre Mercier? As in the industrialist?"

Jennings's rictus smile reappears. "As in Konstatin Böhm's former business partner, and biggest financial donor."

Ansible noses her car out through the crowd around the hotel. Protesters smack her windshield with placards, utterly disinterested in who she actually is. The surrounding reporters are no better behaved. But finally, she's out into the densely woven streets of downtown, travelling past the financial spires and into the poor, run-down suburbs. Then she's through those, moving out to where the money accumulates again in great sprawling estates.

Pierre Mercier lives in a large limestone building ensconced in carefully manicured grounds. At the door, a young man introduces himself—without a hint of irony—as, "Mr Mercier's most personal and personable assistant."

Mercier himself—as sprawling as his estate—waits on his patio, trademark cigar firmly clamped between his teeth. It all feels very staged, very indicative of a fragile ego.

"I imagine," Ansible says, "that you've heard the news."

He stares at his box hedges and rose bushes for a moment. When he finally responds his voice is bearish. "The markets have responded . . . sympathetically."

Ansible isn't sure what she's supposed to say to that.

He turns red-rimmed eyes on her. "My stock is up, yet I am poorer."

She hesitates, then decides that, yes, she's willing to be the asshole. "You stood to lose a lot if the talks are successful."

"This is more than I calculated."

"But unsuccessful talks would be to your advantage."

He shifts his weight at that one, leans forward. "You think my objections to the talks are financial? Do you know what it is I export to East Theora, detective?"

"Enlighten me."

"Cans of laughter, and jars of tears. Specifically of widowed men aged fifty-five to sixty-seven. They take shifts laughing into empty tin cans, which we seal up with wax. Then they go and weep continuously into glass mason jars."

"And is that profitable, Mr. Mercier?"

He waves a hand, indicates the estate. "I take advantage of their insanity, yes, but the thought of normalizing relations with people so abnormal . . .That neither Konstatin nor I could abide."

He leans back but his eyes are still lively. "It seems to me," he says, "that if I were in charge of a case where an opponent of the trade talks was killed by an East Theoran Manus Dei, I might look at an East Theoran who stood to gain a lot from the talks."

"You're very well informed, Mr. Mercier."

The hand waves at the grounds again—all the explanation she's going to get.

"Did you know," he says, "that the East Theoran ambassador leads the largest exportation program East Theora has? Do you know what is going to happen to his profits, detective?"

She chews on that. "Thank you," she says finally. "You've been very helpful."

She's doesn't like Mercier, but doesn't like him for the murder either. Killing a friend to just to make a little more dough is hardly a solid motive for someone as rich as Mercier. Although, she thinks, you never can tell with the rich. They're as bad as junkies sometimes, it's just they're addicted to the cash.

Back at the hotel she finds Jennings again. "Tell me about the ambassador."

"He's as deranged as anyone in the Selazzi Regime." Jennings's vehemence surprises Ansible.

"But he stands to profit from this deal?"

Jennings hesitates. "In a way." In the light from the window her hair looks thin, patchy.

"What way?"

"To the East Theorans, money is just a way of dealing with us. Otherwise, it's basically meaningless to them. They care about currying favors with their gods, with the Selazzi themselves."

The Selazzi—vast abominations rotting, and pulsing, and eternally failing to die far beneath the earth, their psychic extrusions leaking into the nightmares of the Empiricist Empire.

"The ambassador has high standing with one of the Selazzi," Jennings continues. "A successful deal will increase his standing with it, make the standing of other's less meaningful."

"So . . . he'll profit."

"He won't want to talk to you again."

"Well, then it's bad days all round then, isn't it?"

The ambassador expresses his displeasure by making her wait. She expected something more creative from him. He leaves his bodyguard behind too, just bringing the translator. A bold move given the events of the day, or perhaps just a way to show how little she means to him.

She starts talking before the ambassador has a chance to sit down. "You weren't wholly forthcoming with me about your stake in these talks."

He doesn't sit down. He grabs his chair and swings it at her.

She yells, dives away. The translator shrieks, apparently as caught off guard as her.

The ambassador advances, chair held aloft. She flings herself sideways as he smashes it down with stunning force. It comes apart, spattering splinters in a detonation of wooden shrapnel. The seat cushion flaps wildly.

How could someone so scrawny have so much strength inside him, Ansible wonders?

Inside him. Oh shit.

Outside she can hear people yelling.

The ambassador holds two chair legs reduced to stakes. The translator is screaming, high and shrill. She's pulling her gun. If she's wrong about this, this is about to be one hell of an international incident.

The ambassador looms over her. She fires.

He lurches sideways but she wings him, spinning him around and sending him to the floor. They both scramble up, her into a crouch, him onto all fours.

People are bursting into the room, screaming at her.

The ambassador darts forward. She fires again, puts three rounds into his looming head.

They are the eye of the storm—an utterly still pair, while around them security forces from both sides of Theora whirl. The translator is on his knees, shaking and muttering to himself.

Someone puts a gun to the back of her head. She doesn't know if it's someone from her side or theirs. It only matters if she was wrong though.

She wasn't.

The Manus Dei bursts from the ambassador's back in a spray of blood and bone. People scream, shoot. The gun leaves the back of Ansible's head, and she starts firing, but the thing makes a powerful, hundred-handed leap into the air, sailing over everyone's heads, crashing into the still-swinging doors.

She's after it in a flat sprint, but by the time she's shoved through the crowd of bodies and out of the doors, the corridor outside is empty.

She seethes, turns around. Chaos still churns the conference room, but the ambassador's eviscerated body and the quaking translator still sit in the quiet eye of it all.

She grabs the translator. "Why didn't the bodyguard come?"

He stares at her, wild-eyed. Up close, the sheen on his skin looks like plastic. There's an edge near his hairline looking red and raw.

"The shimmer in the eyes is the glow that bakes-"

She rattles him hard. "Translate!"

He swallows, his burnished Adam's apple bobbing. "I don't know. In the ambassador's room? I waited for them both but only the ambassador came out. He told me he didn't need his bodyguard."

Because, Ansible knows, he was already dead.

The bodyguard is gone by the time they toss the ambassador's room. Jennings is there, looking like she's shedding another pound of hair into the room, her skin almost as shiny as the quivering translator who Ansible has dragged there in case he can find anything out of place. She knows she certainly won't. The logic of the room is opaque to her: furniture set on angles perpendicular to her expectations, books spread out in a grid, all open to the thirty-seventh page.

"Tell me more about a Manus Dei," she tells the translator.

He coughs. "In among the gloaming waves I wander..." He shakes his head. "Sorry. I mean, it's a religious vessel, a vehicle for an operator's intent."

"An operator," Ansible repeats. The bodyguard?"

He shrugs.

"These people are fucking monsters!" Jennings kicks at the books in disgust. She seems on the verge of screaming.

Ansible ignores her. "Is it . . . made? Summoned?"

It looks like the sweat is stuck under the plastic sheen on the translator's skin. "It's a ritual. The investment of a piece of the Selazzi into a clay model."

"So, the ritual requires clay?"

"Yes."

"What else?"

"Erm . . ." A set of rapid blinking. "Cans of laughter. Jars of tears."

"Like this?" Jennings stands in the closet holding up a can and a jar. Emblazoned on each is Pierre Mercier's logo.

It would be neater, Ansible thinks, if she didn't get a call on the radio on the way over to Mercier's saying that he'd just reported a break in. It'd make more sense if when they pulled into the estate the most personable of personal assistants had been standing over the bodyguard's dead body, tying up his boss's loose ends.

Instead, Mercier and his assistant are locked in a panic room. Security guards have the bodyguard trapped in a windowless study.

Ansible has West Theoran security pull the bodyguard out. He tries to fight, but the rifles on him settle him down.

"You're under arrest for murder," she tells him.

He sneers at her. "Diplomatic immunity." It sounds like a phrase he's memorized.

"He's right, I'm afraid."

Ansible has arranged another meeting with Jennings. The foreign office woman is looking calmer, as if the ghosts haunting her have taken a step back.

"So, the bodyguard just gets to walk?" Ansible's headache is back.

"East Theoran justice is far worse than anything we can offer." She curls her lip. "Those people are animals."

"You're not the most diplomatic diplomat I've ever met."

Jennings shrugs. "They're not in the room. I don't have to pretend."

"How long were you over there for?"

Jennings shudders. "Six months."

"Undercover?"

Another shudder. "No, it was official. That was the worst of it. They would parade their insanity in front of me. They showed me things they were actually proud of." Her voice is rising. She takes a breath, steadies herself. "Did you," she asks, "arrest Mercier?"

"At what point," Ansible asks her, "when you were over there, did you learn about the Manus Dei?"

Jennings blinks slowly.

"Or maybe a better question," Ansible continues, "is when did you meet the ambassador's bodyguard? Maybe the Manus Dei was his idea. You'll have to explain it to me."

Jennings takes a breath. "What are you talking about?"

"It was easy to like the Ambassador for this," Ansible says. "Böhm cast himself as the villain, and so the natural role for the Ambassador is the avenging hero. Plus he had a vested interest in the deal going through.

She strokes her chin a bit. It's showboating, but she's feeling smug. "Except if the government really thought Böhm could affect the outcome," she says, "would they really have let him attend? Because his failure to derail everything would be a great way to de-fang the mob out there." Ansible points to the window and where the pro-testers still chant.

"But if I didn't bite on the ambassdor," she contines, "well you were there to point me at Mercier. And he's an asshole. It's easy to want to pin this on him as well. And when I didn't quite take the hint, you even had the can and jar as props. That was a nice touch. Except your assassin had failed in his job when he got to Mercier's, hadn't quite sealed the deal."

Jennings looks wild now, her thin face working. "Maybe there was evidence pointing his way," she shouts, "because he's guilty! Maybe the solution is just obvious!"

Ansible sighs. "You know they keep records of who they sell that stuff to, right? I had Mercier look it up. There's not many people in West Theora who buy it. And I checked your bank accounts."

It's so fast, it catches Ansible flat-footed. Jennings breaks for the door at a sprint. But the security guard she posted there catches Jennings by both wrists.

"They're monsters!" Jennings screams as they cuff her. "They're rabid! We have to keep them out!"

"The only thing that mattered to you," Ansible says, more for her own satisfaction than anyone else's, "was that the talks were destabilized."

"We have to keep them out!"

Ansible smooths her hair. "The East Theorans have requested that you be sent over there for the trial," she tells Jennings. "From what I hear, your colleagues are thinking of letting them have you."

Inside the hotel where she orchestrated the murder of three men, Jennings starts to scream.

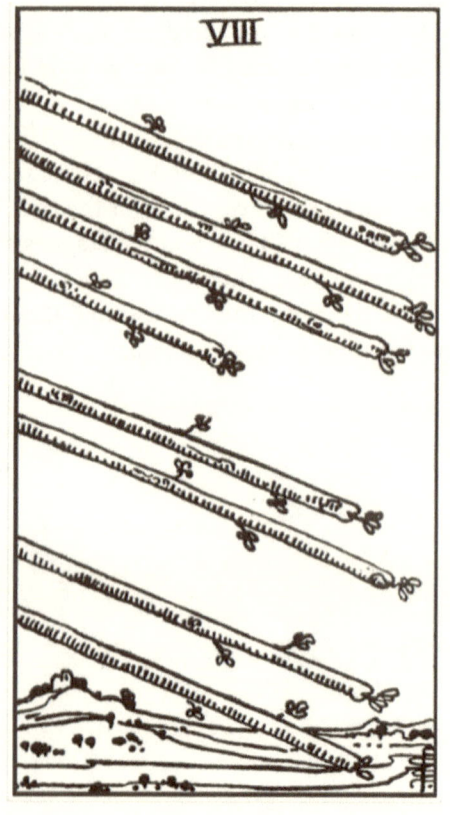

Lakeside

~ A. P. Howell

He stood in the lake between the boat ramp and the dock. Just the same as last night, and so many nights before. Sharon no longer wondered if her eyes were tricking her, if the human shape was merely an illusion of shadows and memory.

The moon was out, bright and full and shining on the water. The lake was just the tiniest bit choppy, animating the edges of the long strip of reflected moonlight. The wind set Sharon's chimes singing and carried the scent of the lake to her nostrils. It wasn't a good scent. The algae bloomed in the August heat, nothing she'd want to drink or swim in but more hassle than danger. The brightly colored patches were easy enough to avoid if you knew to look for them.

Sharon felt like she owned the lake, or at least a part of it, no matter that the deed said the property ended more or less where the water began. She knew the curve of the shoreline, the place where rocks gave way to silt, which of the little island coves would clog with weeds, which channels allowed access and which would cost her a prop blade. And he, too, had become part of the landscape.

His body was a black cutout against the water, limned in silver. She couldn't make out any details of his expression, but she could feel the weight of his gaze.

It didn't bother her, not any more. If he was determined to stand in the water all night, every night, let him. She was not about to sacrifice her view of the moonlit lake. Not tonight, not any night.

Sharon had considered selling the place, her spoils of war, her legal entitlement that was worth so much less than she deserved for what she'd been put through. Take the money and never look back. That would be a kind of victory. But she had fought to remain here, had been so very patient. She deserved to sit here, and did not quite know who she would be if she went elsewhere.

Seven years was a long time to wait, but at least he had not made the sort of will he'd sometimes threatened when at his most angry, drunk, or petty. The local fish and game club would see no windfall, nor would the cousin he'd loved like a brother when they were young.

Seven years was a long time to wait, but the years before had been even longer. Sharon didn't like to think of herself as weak, but apparently she had been, given everything he'd put her through. She could have left—especially early, before so many doors closed, before she became so dependent—but at least she'd become strong in a different way.

Seven years, and all the years since, waiting for a story on the news. An angler with a gruesome catch. A dog retrieving an unexpected bone. No one was searching for him, but the lake wasn't deep.

She wasn't afraid any more. She'd spent too many years afraid. At some point, her heart and resolve had hardened permanently, and the way she'd felt on that night long ago had become her constant reality. Most days, she liked that; and even when she didn't, it wasn't as though she had much choice. Hearts and minds had minds and hearts of their own.

For the longest time, it seemed like he'd stood chest deep, deep enough to swamp waders. But as the years passed it became clear that he was coming closer. The water no longer reached his waist. At some point, he would climb out of the water, moving ever closer to the cabin.

It would take a while for him to make his way out of the lake. Years, based on how long it had taken him to get this close to shore. Then he'd have to walk up the little boat ramp and the switchbacked driveway, or else crawl up a ten foot ridge. He'd have to cross the remaining flat ground to the cabin.

And after that, he'd have to come inside.

If he could've done anything from a distance, surely he would've by now. He'd never been patient with anyone, least of all her.

When he was close enough, well-lit enough, would he look like he had in life, the way he used to look in her nightmares? Or would she see the blood from that last night, his expression one of accusation and surprise?

Sharon's curiosity was dulled, and she had not felt a fight or flight reaction in years.

There was no need to think about events far off in the future. That sort of leisurely attitude was something she'd always liked about the lake. She had plenty of time. And it wasn't like she was going to live forever. Heart disease or cancer might get her before he came anywhere close to the cabin. Sharon was well past the age of resenting genetic predispositions and the frailty of the human body.

She held her mug up in a good-night toast, drained it, and turned off the porch light before retiring to her bed.

KNIGHT of CUPS.

Asylum Cake

~ Eric Witchey

I was the last ghost hunter in the haunted asylum. My three-person crew, Garret, Lindon, and Svetlana, had all bolted by one AM.

Garret first.

We had just put several dozen organic eggs, a monster tub of real butter, and a few gallons of whole milk in the abandoned asylum kitchen. Any real ghostly presence would spoil the eggs, curdle the milk, and make the butter go rancid. I didn't like the low-tech ghost detectors, but enough self-appointed expert viewers had left us follower comments that high-tech tools fritzed when real ghosts made an appearance. We added backup to make them happy. Garret checked the eggs and sniffed the dairy. Into his lapel mic, he said, "1:00:00 AM. The eggs and dairy are fine."

As if his words were an incantation, the disconnected industrial dispose-all started up on its own. I got a five second, wide-eyed night-vision selfie from his head-mounted GoPro before my equipment man turned to me and said, "Screw this shit. I didn't sign up for real ghosts."

He bolted. His custom Electromagnetic Voice Phenomenon (EVP) detector and hand-held infrared camera hit the slick tile floor. To my amazement, neither one shattered. Unfortunately, his night-vision headset went with him.

The equipment in my van caught his footage, but I never saw him or the headset again.

Lindon, my roving cameraman, abandoned us second.

He had just arrived to see what was up with Garret when the double doors to the walk-in pantry opened like jaws. Rusted can, rotted label, and spoiled bean stink poured out on a column of cold air just before an ectoplasmic hand grabbed his loose shirt and pulled him toward the pantry maw.

Static from the EVP on the floor died, and a man's clear, midwestern-accented words sounded out. "Turn on the lights! Turn them on!"

Lindon spun faster than an Olympic diver to break the gooey grip then sprinted even faster than Garret, leaving nothing behind except the echo of his girly scream.

Svetlana, my medium, was made of strong Romani stuff. After watching the tail end of Lindon's encounter and hearing the EVP, she cursed the ghost and me in Russian then took a flask from a hip holster she had worn since I first met her. We had all joked about her belt having more pockets and better stuff than Batman's utility belt.

I thought, Good. holy water. She came prepared.

She had come prepared, and I suppose she might have thought she had brought holy water.

"Vodka," she said. She popped the cap and slammed back a deep swallow like the Ruska Roma she was. She then handed it to me. "Is good. Is for nerves."

After what I experienced in my hour in the Willamette Hills Out-Patient Retreat and Asylum, you bet I hit that flask. For nerves, you know?

I was in the reality YouTuber and general streaming game as a way of sharing my quest to find real ghosts and crowd-sourcing research, but I was the only true believer in my crew. The two guys joined me because hey, reality TV, TikTok Followers, Instagram, and YouTube. For them, identity relevance meant being seen doing things other people hoped were real.

Svetlana hadn't joined us to build a community of channel monkeys feeding on content. In her interview, she said, "I come here because Prababushka . . . How you say?"

"Grandmother?"

"Ah. No. Great Grandmother says to me, 'Go there with that boy.'"

I figured she was either adlibbing script to impress her maybe new boss or coming on to me. I'd had influencer groupies before, and she was kind of hot in an "I'll kick your ass if you piss me off tattooed Russian ninja chick sort of way."

I liked her and her story. I liked her because, well... Because I liked her. I liked her story because the Great Grandmother who told her to interview for the job had been dead for five decades. Combining her hot vibe and the story, I didn't care what her real reasons were.

Even so, when the ancient tank of an industrial cake mixer started up on its own, she calmly handed me her vodka and said, "You nice boy. Not so smart American, but nice. I hope you live." Then, she turned and calmly walked out of the building without another word.

Which put me in the middle of a 1 a.m. dark asylum kitchen listening to rustling in the pantry, a spinning industrial cake mixer, a grinding dispose-all, and, un-expectedly, a never before absolutely clear-voiced EVP monitor.

"Turn on the fucking lights!" the EVP screamed. "Turn on the God-damned LIGHTS!"

Precedents that tell you what to do when encountering real ghosts don't exist. I mean, most of the shit you hear about or see on social media is just made up. Ninety per-cent is scripted to gain followers.

In the olden days before social media, there was that Hans Holzer guy and his friends. In the 1950s and 60s, they did their best to investigate and document. Back in Hans's day, ghost hunters had to be dead serious because they were going to have to live with ridicule and ignomi-ny. Today, all the online and channel-show ghost hunters pretend to use his discovery and documentation meth-ods modified with a few tech updates. A bored popula-tion craves the adrenaline boost of a scream in the dark. Visuals and suspense for media feeds are more import-ant than meeting actual ghosts.

Don't get me wrong. No way I was above a boost in "Like, Subscribe, and Click on the Bell." I had my silver YouTube plaque, and my Insta had 100k followers, and I figured my crew bolting one-by-one would send my Night in the Asylum video viral. From the garnering sponsors perspective, the shoot was already done, but there was no way I could leave without learning more. Like I said, I got into it for real ghosts.

By phone flashlight, I found the light switches next to the swinging metal double doors from the kitchen to the asylum's cafeteria. I tossed the switches—all six of them. The place had been abandoned for over a decade, and Garret and Lindon had assured me the whole facility was completely disconnected from the grid. I didn't expect lights, but I did hope for a response from the ghost/poltergeist/whatever the hell was living out its afterlife in the kitchen and giving such a clear EVP signal.

The lights came on.

Like, there's no power in the building, but the lights came on.

Like, all the lights.

The kitchen lights, the pantry lights, the cafeteria lights, the patient room corridor access lights, and probably all the office and dormitory and rec room lights, too, though I couldn't see them from the kitchen.

In an EVP digital voice I swear sounded profoundly relieved, the box said, "Oh, thank fucking god."

Corny, and a little late, I know, but I was scared, so I fell back on my lame scripted patter. "If there is any presence in this place, any spirit with unfinished business, please make yourself known to—"

The mixer stopped. The dispose-all stopped. The noise in the pantry stopped.

My ears strained for anything reassuring in the silence.

The EVP spoke. "Thanks!"

That made me jump and think it would be a really good time to return Svetlana's flask.

Before I followed my crew, the thing went on. "I've been trying to get someone to turn on those lights for twelve years. Twelve years! I thought I'd go insane. Every damned night, living in terror."

Hand on the flask and eye on the doors, I said, "Uh, okay." My script was scrap. Bravely adlibbing, I asked, "Why?"

The EVP, still on the floor, had a QLED touchscreen. It flashed as the apparition spoke. "You know this is an asylum, right?"

"Uh, yes."

"And you came her to find ghosts because you figured there would be disturbed spirits?"

"Yeah . . . ?"

"Maybe some real nut jobs? Serial killers? Sociopaths? Psychopaths?"

"Maybe. I suppose."

"Idiots. They all come here for that, but it isn't that kind of asylum."

The giant mixer snapped on again, spun the massive twisting, off-center mixing blades through one revolution, and stopped.

A little stunned, I mean I was talking to some kind of disembodied spirit, I asked, "What kind of asylum is it?"

"For rich folks. Phobias, mostly. A few low-intensity personality disorders."

Grasping for some sense of who I was talking to, I asked, "Were you a doctor?"

"Cook."

"You were the cook?"

"Didn't I just say that? Look around, ghost hunter. You're standing in a kitchen. Did you come here because the volleyball court was haunted? The tennis court? The patient rooms?"

"You had a volleyball court here?"

"No." Static squawked from the EVP. "Catch up, man. I made that up to make a point."

I felt silly. The ghost was right. We had packed up the van and driven four hours from Vancouver WA to the middle of nowhere coastal foothills Oregon forest to check out the haunted kitchen stories about the Willamette Hills Out-Patient Retreat and Asylum. "Yeah," I said. "We came to check out the stories about the kitchen."

"It's not rocket science. Kitchen ghost. Cook."

"And the thing with the lights?

"Nyctophobia. Perk of the job. Free therapy. I'm afraid of the dark."

God, I hoped the Wi-Fi tethered recorders in the truck were storing all this. My mic was on. So was my head strapped GoPro. The EVP had been online when Garret bolted, but you never knew if what you believed you were hearing was the same as what the equipment picked up. "Did you die here?"

"Well, duh. Are you a ghost hunter?"

Trying to calm the spirit and get past his snark, I asked, "How?"

"Hobart." The mixer clicked and spun up to a pretty good whining, twisting mix pace.

"Was Hobart a patient?"

The mixer stopped. "Hobart is the company that built the mixer."

I checked out the massive machine bolted to the floor. The metal bowl had wheels and was big enough for me and Svetlana to hide in. The metal paddles that mixed whatever went in that bowl looked like two multi-tined forks the size of tennis rackets spinning and twisting in and out of one another's orbits. "How the hell did that thing kill you?"

"It was installed in the 60s. No safety features."

"You would have had to climb in the bowl. Why would you do that?"

"It was the week we were closing. I still needed therapy, and I was pretty bummed about losing my free appointments."

The reason the ghost was stuck on the mortal plane seemed to be coming into focus. "You suicided."

"Hell, no!"

My plan to calm the spirit wasn't going well. "I'm sorry. Really, I'm sorry."

"Yeah. Sure."

"I'm interested. I want to know what happened."

"You'd be the first."

"I turned on the lights."

The EVP went silent for three of my exploding heart-beats before the cook said, "Baking a goodbye cake for all the staff and patients meant using the big mixer, but I wasn't happy about it."

"An afraid of the dark cook who died baking a cake—that's your story?"

"You wanted a ghost. You found one. Now, you want what? Napoleon? Hitler? Maybe Marie Curie glowing in the dark and cackling?" The mixer stopped. "Selfish much?"

"I'm sorry." And I was. I mean, talking to that ghost was everything I'd hoped for, and everything I said seemed to upset it.

The ghost seemed to sense my sincerity. "Technically," it said, "I died mixing the batter. Gordo Tenston, who called himself The Prankster Orderly, stuck a hand in from the cafeteria and flipped the lights off. He thought that kind of thing was funny, and they couldn't exactly fire him in the last week of operations. The asshole had Borderline Personality Disorder and loved triggering phobias because he had decided they were all faked."

"So the sudden dark scared you to death?"

"I told you. Hobart. Mixer. I was startled. I jumped enough that my hand got caught between the mixer blades. By the time anybody showed up, I was pulled into the batter and beaten into red dye number 2."

That was a little more graphic than I wanted. YouTube might demonetize me if I didn't cut that part, but the cook who died making a goodbye cake was brilliant quirky stuff. Nobody had done anything like it, and I had a real ghost talking to me. Finally. In that moment, I wished Svetlana were still with me. She'd have at least pretended to understand my excitement.

"Fear of the dark, then," I said, "and a goodbye cake."

"Look," the ghost said, "Do you mind if I work while we talk?"

"No."

The pantry started to rattle. The doors opened again, and ingredients started to file out of the closet in a silent Sorcerer's Apprentice sort of floating dance.

I was thinking, I'm so totally going to be rolling in sponsors.

The giant Hobart mixer spun up. A spray hose from the sink stretched out and poured water into the giant metal mixing bowl.

"A cake?" I asked.

"Unfinished business," the cook said. "Twelve years of night terror gives a ghost a craving for a calming ritual. Baking is sort of my thing."

"Why didn't you—"

"Bake in the light? Not how it works. I can't haunt in the daytime, and I'm too scared to bake in the dark. Hell, I can't even move."

"But you rattled the cupboards and touched people and stuff."

"I hid in the pantry, shook in my ectoplasmic skin, and tried to get people to help me."

I supposed that made some sense. "And nobody would turn on the lights?"

"You saw what happened when I tried to get your friends' attention."

"Oh."

I watched the ingredients, including all the eggs, milk, and butter we had brought, mixing for a while then kicked myself for not thinking of setting up more coverage. While the ghost mixed and baked, I went to the van and brought in extra cameras to catch all the footage I could.

Several bowls of different colored icing made themselves while the batter in huge cake pans baked. About three AM, the layers of a massive cake came out of the oven, floated across the kitchen to a counter, and stacked themselves. A spreading spatula rose from a drawer, dipped into icing bowls, and spread sweet goo over the layers.

"The asylum is empty," I said. "Who's going to eat all this?"

"You," the cook said, "for one. Others will show up. Bake a cake, people show up to eat it. Of course, I've never gotten this far before, so maybe not."

I checked my cameras and recorders.

"As thanks for the eggs and dairy, here's some advice," the ghost said, "Set up a couple cameras in the cafeteria."

I did. If you're a ghost hunter, you don't argue when a ghost gives you ghost hunting advice.

The finished cake, a gorgeous thing decorated with marbled swirls of brilliant colors and a single sparkling red calligraphy word, "Goodbye," rose from the counter and floated to the cafeteria doors.

Instinctively, I pushed the doors open.

"Thanks," the cook said.

"No problem."

The cake passed through and settled itself on a table. A moment later, a cake knife the size of my arm floated out of the kitchen and poised over the cake.

As soon as the blade touched icing, the entire cafeteria filled with ghostly forms: amorphous spectral wraiths, transparent shambling people in hospital gowns, white-coated doctors and nurses, a couple of janitors, and a handful of casually dressed ghosts who might have just walked in off the street.

"They all died here?"

The cook said, "No, but they all know how important it is to celebrate healing."

Trying to make sense of the confusing gathering of specters, I said, "Your intention in the baking determined who showed up?"

"You're trying too hard," the cook said. "Just enjoy the party. Have some cake."

The cake sliced itself. The assembled ghosts ate and chatted and clapped. As the cake disappeared, they even sang oldie '80s disco and '90s alternative rock songs like bored old people on a European tour bus.

I caught every detail in glorious 4k digital.

When the last ghost finished the last piece of cake, all the apparitions disappeared. A loud, metallic clank shook the walls of the asylum, and the building went dark.

In that first moment of absolute darkness and silence, I discovered my own loneliness in my lost connection to the nyctophobic baker. "Cook?" I asked the silent darkness.

No response.

By the light of my phone, I made my way back to the kitchen. "Cook?"

The EVP monitor cast a low, silent glow on a few floor tiles.

Behind me, a door squeaked.

I jumped and turned.

Svetlana strode in, her hand-held utility belt flashlight burning a white, high-intensity LED beam through the darkness.

Grateful for her stoic company, I said, "They're gone."

"They?"

"The cook, the doctors, the patients."

"For decade," she said.

"They were here. I talked to them. Filmed them."

"Great Grandmother say ghosts only can talk at night."

"It is night. They were just here."

"Is dawn," she said. "Sun up now. No window here."

"Oh."

She swept her light around the kitchen. The beam stopped on a top hat-sized triple-layered cake bearing a calligraphy message. "Thank you. Fill the darkness with light."

Svetlana asked, "You bake?"

I said, "No."

"Ah," she said. "Outside, Svetlana is walking on road. Great Grandmama appears. She says to me, 'You go share boy's cake.'"

"Really?"

She smiled, nodded, and crossed to the cake.

As morning light filtered through the windows of the asylum and a diffuse glow reflected into the kitchen, Svetlana and I enjoyed the ghost cook's gift. After the last delicious bite, she said, "We are done here?"

"Yeah. They're not coming back."

"Okay." She holstered her flashlight and gave me a sweet, icing-covered peck on the cheek.

A week later, Svetlana and I argued over whether to let Great Grandmother take the night shift driving, agreed to try it, set the destination to our next investigation, and posted the asylum video.

Comments poured in, as they do...

RealityGeek49 10 minutes ago
Obviously fake. Production values too high.

SpookSpaz12 13 minutes ago
Cook voice a hired actor. Heard them on anime.

SvenTheZombieSlayer 1 hour ago (edited)
More Svetlana. Less moron who thinks cake is cool.

> Reply: **Prababushka** Sad child. Your grandmother Sophia taught you read. She weeping.

NEXT VIDEO: Ghosting Hunting at the Heceta Head Lighthouse with Svetlana, Prababushka, and American Boy.

QUEEN ᴏꜰ PENTACLES

From or Belonging to the Spring People

~ Kiya Nicoll

The girl stood on tiptoe, leaning over the velvet rope to peer into the case, not quite reaching forward to put her hands on the glass. She was albino, perhaps, though her skin lacked the rosy undertones one might expect, and her eyes were an ice blue that matched the bluish shading of her cascade of perfectly straight white hair. Her dress was a green so dark as to seem almost black, and the string of simple red beads she wore as a necklace seemed stark and bloody.

"Don't touch the glass," the guard said.

The girl pirouetted on one foot to look at him, to look him up and down, and then laughed, and spread her arms, dancing into a near-run and wheeling around one case, then another, like a hawk spiraling on a thermal, before she darted out into the hall and was gone. The private communications crackled to keep an eye out for her, and her recklessness, and to scold any parent that seemed attached to her, but she did not reappear.

She was the first, or at least the first that anyone noticed.

The next was a man, at least seven feet tall and broad in the shoulder, brown as an oak and hair dreadlocked into shaggy orange pollen strands. He loomed over the glass cases, looking down at them from above, his chuckle rumbling like thunder as he leaned to read the labels.

When another man slipped in, tiny, fawn-colored and black-eyed, the giant turned to him and greeted him with a booming, "Brother!" that made him jump, eyes going wide and startled. The big man crossed over to him in two strides, setting a hand on his shoulder, and steered him around to the case on the end. "Tell me, brother, do you think it's authentic?"

The skittish little man allowed himself to be rearranged, and peered at the label. "From or belonging to the Spring People," he said aloud, and then said, "Well." He hopped in place once, then twice, and on the third the giant caught him in the air and held him suspended so that he could look down at the necklace. "Hmmmm. Put me down, brother."

"Well, what do you think?"

"It's the eye beads that have me particularly skeptical," he said, in the tone of one who really ought to have spectacles to take off and polish while theorizing. "I'd expect more ambiguity about whether or not they're also roses."

The giant laughed, leaning back, his hands on his hips, as if he had just been told a tremendous joke. "You know, you're right."

"Of course I'm right," he said, peering up high enough to strain his neck. "You wouldn't have asked me to look otherwise." He staggered a little when the other clapped him on the shoulder, but did not stumble into the case or back against the velvet rope. "The greens are quite good for them, though."

"They are. The yellowish sheen there is like that girl I was seeing that time."

The small man rolled his eyes. "I know, you like the Dawn ones."

"Regardless of season!" boomed the giant, laughing, but the smaller man was back to studying the necklace, frowning. "What's wrong now, brother?"

"Oh, just thinking that if the greens are particularly suited to a Spring Person of the Dawn, the reds are more suited to one of the Night and that's an odd combination."

"Is it? Does it have colors that suit the entire daily wheel?"

"Pick me up again, brother," he said, and the giant obliged. "The shimmering golds might do for a child of the Midday, and the olives for Twilight, but that dark green there seems to be a duplication of Night. And of course there are minor times left unmarked, but they often are, that's hardly indicative. The reds could be Autumn, too, though, and that tangles the whole thing up in briars."

The big man did not put him down.

"Brother?"

"I was wondering if it had Sun, Moon, and Stars, in your judgement, actually," he said, thoughtfully.

With a frown, the other said, "Not sure. I could make the argument, but it's a bit muddier than is typical. If

the dark green is Night without Stars, the red is still per-
plexing."

"Night with Moon? On the tulips? Or possibly the Sun
at Night in Spring?"

He grunted. "Put me down, brother. I'm stumped."

"Let's go have a beer, then." On that note, they left, in
amiable company, and the other visitors to the exhibit
clustered, briefly, around the piece in dispute, to verify
what they had overheard, and to try to make sense of it.

It was two days before another of the curious museum visitors came to look at the necklace. She leaned on
a cane, her stooped shoulders shrouded in a cape made
of soft black feathers, her hair curling over it, this lock
auburn, that lock silver, like maple leaves edged in frost.
Her face had a certain agelessness to it, crow's feet around
eyes that seemed full of laughter, yes, but neither terribly
wrinkled nor terribly worn, and she said, "Hmmm," to
the glass case, and then started to laugh.

"Why is that lady laughing?" asked a child, fist knotted
in her mother's coat to tug for attention.

The woman turned, the base of her cane making a sharp
noise against the floor as she did, a noise that turned
heads. She lowered herself like she could fold down-
wards and said, "Schöner Streich," and then frowned.
"Nein, no . . ." It took her a moment to figure out what
language she wanted, and it still came accented with a
German that had an odd, mincing lilt to it, as if the entire
concept of words was worth mockery. "It is a good joke.
A beautiful joke? More ways than one. So I laugh."

The child frowned at that, scuffing one foot against the floor. "What sort of joke?"

"Morgenstern." The old woman stood, unfolding again, hands straining against the head of the cane. "No. Lucifer? A morning-star sort of joke."

"What's a morning-star joke?" asked the child, and her mother tried to hush her, inspiring only recalcitrance.

"Nein, no, I do not mind," said the woman, with a wave of her hand. "Here is the joke: one who brightly burns, who high above the sun flies, but cannot escape, and back he falls, gone, invisible. Poof! And those who their aim set when the morning star is high, they, too, are lost, into the sun to follow."

"That doesn't seem very funny to me." There was an intense edge of stubbornness in the tone, that bordered on sullenness.

"Should you become as old as I," the woman said, with a curl of a smile at some private joke that made her eyes dance, "perhaps the humor of it you will see. The morning star returns, you know, but humans never learn."

"How old are you?" demanded the child, and her mother gasped. "Never learn what?"

The woman laughed again, and answered, "Old enough to know secrets," with a smile that suggested she had quite a few of them hoarded up, upon which she slept like a smug cat.

The child refused to be cowed. "What sort of secrets?" she demanded, with a little stomp of one foot. Her mother stammered an apology and tried to drag her away, but the woman just chuckled and said, "I do so enjoy young humans."

"Why?"

"You have not yet grown into being conventional and afraid," she said, putting her head to one side and smiling that smug little smile, like she was searching through her vault of treasures, letting them slide over her hands like beads to select one that she might consider handing over. "Come, I will whisper you a secret in your ear, if you can convince your mother to let you."

"Mom," she said, dragging out the word in the pleading note of children possessed of a great desire.

"All right, go ask," her mother said, in the defeated tones of someone who does not care to have this fight right now, particularly not in the middle of a crowded museum exhibit. "I'll be right here keeping an eye on you."

The motley-haired woman said, with grand amiability, "Oh, I haven't stolen any children away for years, I don't have a place to store them these days," and then leaned down again, shifting her cane so she could keep her balance.

"What's the secret?" hissed the girl.

"When someone a favor asks, and does not their name offer? Then is the time to be very cautious. Some people play tricks, like the one who had that necklace brought here."

The girl looked up, eyes narrowing. "What's your name?" she asked immediately.

The woman laughed, head thrown back, and then said, "You may call me Hulda, child."

"Thank you, Hulda." She frowned, with a judiciously skeptical look, and then said, "Hmmmm," and marched back to her mother's side.

Her mother took her hand, firmly, and asked, "Why are you making that face?"

"She didn't say it was her name. Just that that's what I could call her."

The older woman straightened, chortling. "Such a clever girl," she murmured, and then said, more loudly, "When the Queen of Summer hears the gossip, it will be quite a show. But perhaps a show you don't want to see." She gave the necklace another long, studious look, and then made her way out, still chuckling.

Again, the museum staff made note; a Queen of Summer who promised to make trouble probably ought to be prepared for, though nobody was at all certain what to expect of her. It had become something of a game, by this point, to collect the stories of the peculiar visitors who studied that case in particular: the two identical children, dressed in grey with trailing sleeves like the wings of swallows, who trilled comments to each other in a language nobody recognized and then chased each other out of the museum in darting swoops; the girl with the shockingly yellow hair, wearing a ruffled shirt that was streaked with purple and white, who read the label and laughed uproariously; the big man who stood for hours, motionless as an exhibit himself, stone-faced and with crystalline-pale eyes shocking against the darkness of his skin. They debated whether the little crowd of short fat people who resembled nothing so much like a collection of mixed nuts in their shades of brown, wrinkled like almonds or even pecans, was another such apparition, but while those guests were quite interested in the necklace and talked quietly among themselves about it, they spent more time in front of the display of cups and forks.

None of that prepared them for the blue woman.

She was not particularly tall, but despite that she loomed, her clothes billowing turbulently around her in whorls of grey and ultramarine, whipping to white at the edges. Her hair was swept up into plumes and cascades, green and blue and grey, and her skin was genuinely blue, sky blue, summer sky blue.

There were fewer people in the exhibit, at least, so she swept to the obvious case without catching anyone in her undertow. She read the label, lifted her chin in obvious disapproval, and sniffed once, before turning and walking back out again. Her wake filled with eddies of murmurs and exclamations, and appropriate calls were made to management.

The days after the blue woman had visited were tense ones. Not by anyone's deliberate choice; it seemed more that the air in the museum had that electric sense of potential, something waiting to break open, though it lacked clarity as to when or how. There were no further strange guests, or at least not any that distinguished themselves from the milling visitors. The most remarkable thing anyone noticed was a sulky teenaged girl in a grey hoodie who spent the afternoons in the exhibit, hands in her pockets and watching the people more than the displays.

Midway through the next week, a man arrived, thin and straight and upright as a sunbeam, wearing white robes that shimmered with the intensity of a mirage dancing over hot stone. His hair was long and golden under a thin, precise circlet, his eyes a vivid and unquenchable green. He glided rather than walked to the case containing the necklace, and bent his head just the slightest amount so that he might read the label. "This," he said, and somehow everyone hearing him knew it to be true, "is incorrect."

"Who are you?" asked a guard, stepping forward.

The man made of angles and light turned towards him, and did not speak, but everyone present understood, for a fleeting instant, the vast spinning angles of space, the pole bent sunwards for long enough for a breath before sweeping on, the dancing orchestra of planets and moons arrayed in their many chords, tracing ellipses in the breath of stars, angles and arcs all made of light. This, too, was a burst of noonlight shining upon white rocks undappled by shade, and the sharp brine smell of the sea.

"You can't just be at them," said a voice, a swaggering voice belonging to a swaggering man. "You have to use mouth noises to communicate." He was broad and red-brown, tall but not overwhelmingly so, his muscularity softened by his paunch. While he also wore a circlet, it was not precise and elegant, but rather a coiled tangle of oak leaves, golden heads of grain, and some sort of red-dish purple berry, from which swept two sharply point-ed horns in a manner that suggested that he might have grown them himself, even as every onlooker was certain that that was obvious nonsense.

The pillar of a man turned towards him. "It is impre-cise."

"You are hopeless." He heaved a tremendous sigh. "Let me translate a moment, I believe he wanted to say that he can be known as, let's approximate, Stilled Sun in Quartz At Noon, Prince Consort to the Queen."

"And who are you?"

"You can call me Frank."

The shining man turned upon Frank a gaze of burning disapproval and sniffed once.

"What?"

Eyebrows like sundogs arched upwards.

"It's hardly my fault you have no discernible sense of humor," Frank grumbled. "And I do intend to be."

The other sniffed again.

"I suppose it's for the best you're too good to actually talk, that language would probably turn half of them into frogs," he snapped back. "Or something worse."

A twist of the hand, a curl of a smile.

"Ugh," Frank declared. As the other man lifted his chin slightly in apparent triumph, he pivoted on his heel and bowed, spreading his arms wide, and said, "My fair Queen."

The victory fled from the pillar's face as he turned, be-latedly, to incline his head with elegant formality, even as

Frank stepped forward and accepted the Queen's hand in his own, bowing over it to plant a kiss on the back.

"My dear consort," she said.

A flicker of displeasure crossed the other man's impassive face. "He has told them to call him Frank."

"Has he?" The Queen seemed amused, more than anything. "I suppose he is." She offered her other hand to Stilled Sun in Quartz At Noon, Prince Consort to the Queen. "But it does not please you, my love."

Afterwards, nobody could agree what she had looked like. When one person spoke of her shockingly bonfire red hair, another frowned and said her hair had been black, and others argued about whether it had been a metallic gold or like beach sand. Her eyes were definitely vibrant and stunning, but whether they were clear summer sky blue, or luminous green, or even yellow was a topic of dispute. They did not bother fighting about whether her gown was green or blue or red, not when they could occupy themselves in endless debate about whether her crown was made of wheat wrought in gold, or crystal that refracted rainbows around her, or had the horns of a stag worked with silver. Her skin might have been golden, or pale green, or a velvety black that glittered faintly as if she were made of stars.

Everyone agreed that she was compelling, that she was beautiful, that she was terrifying.

"It does not," said the shaft of light shaped into a man, as if the Queen were not a force that interrupted all thought, as if he might carry on a conversation with her about his grievances as a matter of the perfectly ordinary.

"And how did you introduce yourself?" purred the Queen. "Did you?"

"I told them who I am," he replied, with a little prim huff.

"You gave them your name?" Her humor turned thunderous, and she seemed to grow taller. "Knowing the risks, you gave them your name?"

Frank glanced at the other consort, and then laid a hand gently on her arm and said, "To be fair, my Queen, they could barely comprehend it, let alone pronounce it. You know how he is about the mouth noises." His other hand shaped itself into a squawking bird's beak, thumb tapping the fingertips, mocking the concept of sound.

There was a moment where she turned on him, where it seemed there might be some incomprehensible act of violence, and then she laughed. "The mouth noises, yes," she said, and the hurricane was gone, leaving everything windswept but miraculously undamaged. "You are indeed correct."

He bowed, just slightly. "My Queen." He looked up as he bowed, meeting the gaze of the pale shining man, who gave him a slight, small nod, curt and acknowledging.

"Show me the necklace," she said, then.

"The label is incorrect." Nonetheless, he pointed, one slender finger aimed at the case.

The Queen shook her head, amused, and swept past them both to study it. "I do remember this piece," she said. "It was given to—oh, who was she, do either of you recall? She was of our court, of course."

Stilled Sun in Quartz At Noon tilted his head, and deigned to say, "She was a midday child."

"Like yourself," the Queen agreed. "Though much later in the season, I believe, not a solstice girl."

Frank drummed his fingers on his chin, twirling a lock of his beard around them. "Beech tree, I believe. And the colors did suit her."

"Even as she turned red in the autumn," agreed the Queen, with a little shake of her head. "A pity. As mortal as her tree, she was." She waved a hand. "We must correct the sign, at least."

"Do you wish to reclaim the necklace?"

"The mortals made it, and the one with a claim to it is centuries gone," she said. "But this is—" she left it unfinished, for long enough that the predictable consort grew uncomfortable enough to say, "Incorrect," so that she could turn to bestow a smile upon him.

Most of the patrons had shifted to one side, where they could watch the strange guests without grand risk of interference. The Queen lifted her chin and crooked a finger at a guard, saying, "Please, fetch someone with authority. We must speak with them."

There was nothing possible but obedience, though the guard hesitated a moment before one said, "I will keep order." Thusly, if not reassured, at least affirmed that the man made of straight lines and undeniable facts would stand guard in his place, the guard hurried off. Certainly, none of the museum visitors seemed likely to challenge him, even the little cluster that was pinned between them and the wall with no route to edge around towards the larger group of people. The teenaged girl among them chewed gum ostentatiously and somehow, despite everything, managed to look unimpressed.

The guard returned promptly, curator in tow, and reclaimed his position.

The Queen turned, head cocked slightly to one side, and said, "Your sign is incorrect." She flicked her fingers imperiously. "Fix it."

The curator was a short woman, somewhat round, with grey hair in loose curls, and she met the gaze of the Queen and said, "The sign is as accurate as we know how to make it, ma'am. If you have information regarding its provenance, we would be happy to review the documentation."

Frank whistled sharply through his teeth, but the Queen simply smiled. "I see," she said, with a purr in her voice. "The owner of the piece was not of the Spring court, but the Summer. I knew her, in passing, of course." A little languid wave of the hand encompassed the span of years casually. "Sweet girl. A mortal made the bauble for her, after a dalliance."

"I see," the curator said, continuing to stare up over the rims of her glasses.

"You do not believe me?"

"I cannot change the labels in the museum on the mere say-so of a visitor," she said. "It would be chaos."

"The sign is incorrect," said Stilled Sun in Quartz at Noon, though his voice wavered, slightly, in the manner of one who also did not approve of chaos, and who could well be swayed by that concern.

"Even if I grant that, I would need to be able to support it to others," the curator said. "And I am certain that people as important as yourselves would not wish to be placed on call to answer questions."

The Queen chuckled. "I see. But the sign must be changed."

"Find me a means by which I can, and I will see to it," the curator said, with stubbornness.

"You dare make demands of me?" Storms returned to the Queen's manner, as if the eye of the hurricane was now past and the fury returning.

She lifted her chin. "You make demands of me, ma'am."

Both consorts took a step back, not certain what the Queen was about to do, but the teenager in the grey hoodie stepped forward into the space they vacated, and put back the hood.

She was not a girl, suddenly, but a fox, standing on hind legs, tall as the girl had been, wearing a grey hooded robe embroidered with silver flowers and a silver circlet worked with buds that shimmered faintly green and white. "I witness," she said, sharp teeth and tongue somehow able to form words. "You challenge a Queen on her own lands, Summer."

The Queen of Summer whirled to face the fox. "Who are you to interfere?"

The fox tipped her head to one side and smirked, somehow, her features twisting with wry humor. "I am what

I am, that leaps and sprouts and appears, all unexpected, and I, like a cat, can spot a Queen."

"Her?" The Queen's finger jabbed at the curator.

"Did you not feel the power by which she held her ground? You are in her domain, after all."

"She speaks truth," said the shining consort.

"Spring," said Frank. "You are riddling again."

The fox laughed. "Do you like this face?" she asked him.

"I've liked others better," he rumbled. "But I know you, no matter what face you put on."

The fox tapped her nose with one finger. "Ah, but you did not know me when I was the mortal girl, did you?"

"I did not, but I also was not looking. My fair Queen held my attention, after all."

"Flatterer," said the Queen, somewhat mollified.

"I merely speak the truth, my beloved," he replied.

The fox rolled her eyes. "Honestly," she said, and tapped one foot, and then said, "Do you happen to know if the mortal who crafted it named it?"

"What?"

"Was it given a name?"

"I do not know," said Stilled Sun in Quartz at Noon, when the Queen looked at him.

Frank shook his head. "I'm unaware of a name, myself."

"So the people who named it are of the court of this queen." The fox pointed at the curator. "And they have named it 'From or Belonging to the Spring People'.

Which means it is mine, not yours." She drew herself up taller, straightening until she matched the height of the Queen of Summer, and her predator's smile grew sharper and hungrier. "And even Queens cannot dispute the power of names. Can we, Summer?" Her hand was now holding a staff or scepter, a stalk that flowered into a spike of cascading rosy-purple bells, and despite her bestial features she had taken on a potent majesty of her own.

"You have a potent glamour, Spring, to hide from me," said Summer.

"Ah, even when they expect me, nobody is quite certain when I will arrive," laughed the fox. "But come, let us take our discussion away from prying mortal eyes."

The Queen of Summer sniffed, and said, "Fine," before saying, fiercely, to the curator, "I shall return."

Spring smiled as sweetly as her fangs would allow. "Unless you yield, of course, in which case the item will remain in my domain, as it is named to be."

The curator stepped back to let them go, first the Queen of Summer, hand in hand with both consorts, and then the fox, her glorious tail swishing behind her as she went. Once they were safely away, she let out a breath and said, to nobody in particular, "Perhaps if we added 'Origin disputed' they won't come back."

ACE of CUPS.

B. waterways

~ Erik Kollmer

As my head prattles against Father's station wagon window to the cadence of the engine, I picture a massive green-scaled, three-headed snake sliding out of the wheatfields onto the single-lane road Father and I trace daily. Maybe it could grab the station wagon with its fangs and jostle it like a helpless cybernetic rabbit. Father would scream and I would laugh because that would be the most exciting thing that has ever happened to us.

The wheatfields have surrounded me my entire existence. The golden grain occupies every square meter that is not a building nor road in Damsel. A common point of conversation among families and neighborhoods is when children have their first inquisition as to what is deep within the wheatfields, colloquially called "W. moments". Ask any other nineteen-year-old what they remember about their W. moment, and they will respond with a scratch of the head and a shrug of indifference. It sears my heart.

"Lucina, you do understand how important today is for me, correct?" Father's apprehensive tone drags me back to the confines of the station wagon. He grips the steering wheel so firmly that his veins look ready to escape his skin. "Please be courteous and kind to everyone at the Community Center, especially Mr. Wingal. He has . . ."

"A silvery handlebar mustache and abnormally long eyelashes. His color is lime green, #3CFA3E. No child because he's on the Council. I remember him from the last Exhibition."

Father expels a soft sigh, then wipes his brow with the sleeve of the only tweed jacket he owns. It is a darker shade of burgundy, #6C011C, specifically matching my dress. Without it, there would be no other way to identify us as parent and child.

I turn my attention back to the wheat blurring together outside. A transmission tower looms over its agrarian subordinates, asserting its industrial dominance as electricity cackles through its wires.

The Community Center is a unique building. Many parents bring their children here after their W. moment to show them the parking circle, as it is the only piece of road in Damsel that defies the town's cartesian street grid. Once inside the Center, guests have the choice of entering either the theater or the ballroom. Of course, this is an Exhibition, so Father and I proceed into the theater and find our assigned seats. As I sit down, the rigid wooden slats rib my exposed back, but I've convinced myself that these seats are uncomfortable by design. As more people fill the theater, it becomes noticeably redolent of sun-kissed wheat.

As soon as the last seat in the theater is occupied, the audience's eyes snap towards the screen at the front of the room. It is a perfect square, 1300 pixels by 1300 pixels, mounted in front of a backdrop of gray curtains. In the center of the screen, the standard preliminary message is spelled out in blue pixels:

B. waterways. Iteration 4003029.
Designed by Resident 6C011C-1.

The audience blinks, and an image with a top-down aerial view of three parallel aqueducts appears on the screen, a thin coating of water flowing across the top of each. Underneath the three aqueducts is a riverbed, which disappears off the top and bottom edges of the image. Then, everyone in the theater begins to stand and clap with an unbridled passion. A spotlight showers down onto the seat next to mine. Whether Father was crying before they displayed his iteration on the screen, I am unsure. I stand up and perform the customary hug, then wipe Father's tears away with my thumbs for sentimental flair. I disgust myself.

At the previous Exhibition a month ago, a woman received a similar standing ovation for changing the pixel that is part of the central aqueduct's wall from a dry, dirty shade of brown (#bb5101) to a slightly darker, earthy brown (#934306). Father had essentially mirrored this color change at pixel (635, 799), which was part of the leftmost aqueduct's wall.

"Brilliant choice, Maxwell! Brilliant!" a gaunt-looking woman in purple drab says behind me, still furiously clapping.

Another woman from a couple rows back joins in. "Such poise in selection, and such beauty in parallelism!"

"This is one of the most intelligent iterations I've seen in quite some time." Over Father's shoulder, I catch a glimpse of Mr. Wingal. My self-loathing only grows as I force a smile and extend my hand to the man outfitted with a pair of lime green circle-framed glasses. He shakes my hand with a mix of tenderness and assurance that, to my displeasure, puts me at ease. Father then turns and clasps Mr. Wingal's other hand in both of his. "Mr. Wingal, I hope this iteration is everything you've been hoping for."

Mr. Wingal grins. "Maxwell, your work is incredibly insightful. Many of the Council and I thought you would return to the contemporary trend of darkening the water pixels, but your adaptation of Gretchen's recent wall-focused idea underscores something . . . awe-inspiring I couldn't quite pinpoint before. Surely you will be remembered forever as one of the early adopters of dirt-brown wall pixelism. A renaissance is afoot!"

I watch as Mr. Wingal's words dismember Father. He staggers back from Mr. Wingal, and I notice a feral smile creep into the seams of Mr. Wingal's mouth. I pity them both.

Feigning affection has never been an issue for me, but I cannot bring myself to express appreciation for a process I find revolting. "Mr. Wingal, why do grafters only change *B. waterways* one pixel at a time? Is there some sort of rule around it?"

Mr. Wingal's eyelashes recoil as far away from his pupils as his eyelids permit. "Lucina . . . are you truly your father's daughter?"

My question also snaps Father out of his torpor. "Mr. Wingal! Please, for the love of Damsel, forgive my daughter. She doesn't quite understand the parameters of grafting yet."

"I see," Mr. Wingal says. He brings his thumb and forefinger up to the corner of his mustache, simultaneously pulling at and twirling the left end. "Let's do this. Lucina, for the Exhibition next month, you shall be in charge of grafting *B. waterways.*"

Father and I slowly turn towards each other, our faces paralyzed with an unholy mélange of horror and shock. Father places his hand on my shoulder to steady himself, then turns to Mr. Wingal.

"With all due respect, Mr. Wingal, I do not believe she is ready for such an important task," he says, quivering.

"Maxwell, I appreciate your concern, but I have made my decision. I trust Lucina will surprise each and every one of us," Mr. Wingal declares, pursing his lips and narrowing his eyes in my direction. "With that, I must bid you both adieu. Maxwell, congratulations again on a job well done."

☉

The silence hanging in the station wagon is finally pierced by the crackling of wheels on gravel. A soft *tunk* floats into the night air as the car's lights turn off. We sit in the darkness, staring straight ahead at our house, the wheatfields an omnipresent backdrop.

"Tell me why you don't think I'm ready," I finally say.

Father clears his throat with a practiced *ahem*. "I'm trying to protect you, Lucina. There are millions of pixels to choose from on top of millions of color palettes. The combinations scale exponentially. Six months passed until I realized how to best improve *B. waterways* for the future, inspiring others to find the beauty in the miniscule. For you to do the same in only one month, and at your age . . . I just don't want you to begin your life labeled a *derivative*." He whispers the final word with sacrilegious precision.

"It did *not* take you six months to decide on which pixel to change!" I exclaim. "You knew which one you were going to pick the instant you were appointed for this iteration seven months ago. The rest of the time you just spent second guessing yourself."

Father stares at me, mouth agape. "Lucina, I . . ."

"You're afraid to ask the bigger questions, Father. You always have been. How did *B. waterways* even come to be if no one in Damsel has ever seen water? Not a single person understands its physics. The concept of water is so abstract to us that we admire it initially, but have you ever wanted to actually *experience* water? How it might actually *degrade* the aqueducts over time, changing B. waterways as we know it?"

Father goes quiet, staring blankly at his palms in his lap. He begins to knead his thumbs together. "Lucina, you're really beginning to worry me. All I ask is for you to make me proud at the next Exhibition."

I kick open the passenger door and step out into the darkness. *It's only now he pays attention to what I have to say.* "Whether I make you proud is your choice," I mutter, shutting the station wagon door with more force than the old car would have liked. As I walk towards the front door, my fingers rub the middle of my bare back and make acquaintance with the impressions the theater seat left etched into my skin. They always linger longer than I expect.

It is only when I reach my bedroom that I allow myself to laugh uncontrollably. Defiant as I am, the opportunity to have an Exhibition all to myself is surreal. For as long as I can remember, I have partaken in the ritual of Exhibitions, but only out of reluctant compliance. Month after month, each iteration tampers with my soul, tempting me to bury my W. moment in a reality plagued with mundanity and the people who proliferate it.

I stare at my posterless bedroom wall, dilate my pupils, and allow Father's version of *B. waterways* to project itself through my eyes. I then tap my right temple to allow my eyes to move freely around the image. They instinctively dart to Father's most recent change at pixel (635, 799), where Mr. Wingal declared a "renaissance is afoot." I shudder. *Could changing one pixel in an image really be the genesis of an entire art movement?* I focus on the other wall pixels around Father's chosen one and use my pupils to draw a virtual perimeter. In my head, I calculate the hex code of the average color across the different shades of brown: #66484a. I search my memory for what I learned in my browns class in school, and recall that #66484a is a red-tinged brown. The color of Father's pixel, #634547, is only slightly darker. *Fitting for him to take as small a risk as possible. He didn't even try changing the color to something more interesting.*

Despite all my misgivings with Father's work, I thought I would have a better idea about what I wanted to add to *B. waterways.* My teachers in school had always dictated that Exhibitions are solely about improving the aesthetic appearance of the whole image. At my core, I always knew that my iteration would break that unspoken rule. But now that I finally had the chance to do so, I found myself struggling to come up with what exactly would establish me as a derivative.

What's beneath the wheatfields?

The thought felt internal, as if something dormant had just awakened within me. An incredible compulsion overcomes me. Whether this thought is going to drive me to madness or inspiration, I am unsure. But I soon find myself walking barefoot in the backyard towards the seemingly impenetrable wall of yellow grain. A friendly full moon assists my hands as they begin to dig at the base of one of the stalks.

About three hand-lengths deep, a cool liquid greets my fingers. I bring my hand back out of the hole and see that my fingers are covered in a viscous, dark liquid. I begin to tremble uncontrollably. *Is this . . . water?* Knowing that I can only verify the color under proper light, I dash back across the lawn and wrap my forearm around the back-yard doorknob to open it without tainting the handle.

Under my bedroom light, the dark liquid becomes a deep shade of crimson. From a quick calculation, I can tell it is, on average, #a81117. This is not water. My senses continue to investigate: a soft, metallic scent. A thick texture that does not disappear as I trace my finger along my arm.

Shadowy notions of despair begin to crawl into the back of my consciousness. The Council could have invented this ink to brand those who had the derivative idea of digging through the wheatfields. While only a moment ago being a derivative seemed like liberation, feeling this viscous substance seep into the cracks of my skin makes me pause and consider a new potential reality: social exile.

I consider showing Father, but decide that confiding in him is the same as telling all of Damsel. Instead, I return to the backyard and try wiping my hands on the lawn. To my delight, the crimson liquid begins to adhere to the grass, and I direct my hands to make large sweeping motions, turning them over intermittently to eliminate the foreign substance. After verifying the cleanliness of my fingers and palms by moonlight, I return to my bedroom. *B. waterways* is still projected on the naked wall.

Fear not, Lucina.

An overwhelming sensation of warmth reverberates throughout my entire body. Once again, its source feels entirely internal. The very fiber of my being tells me the sensation can only be one thing: unconditional love. I try calling out to the source with my thoughts.

Are you my savior?

The only reply is the humming of the power lines that pass close to my bedroom window. I cast an unwavering gaze at *B. waterways*, allowing the image to etch itself into my eyeballs. I shut my eyes tight and allow the patterns of light to appear on the back of my eyelids.

Fear not, Lucina.

Mr. Wingal's condescending smile no longer feels as condemning. The opinions of the Exhibition audience no longer fetter me. I try to explain away every possibility that this overpowering sensation could be some type of ploy by the Council to let my guard down. And yet, it is as if this notion had always been present within me, simply waiting to be untapped.

Is that you, Mother?

Whoever is responsible for the sensation does not respond. A pang of loneliness shoots through me, but is quickly erased once I flutter open my eyes. *B. waterways* is not the same as when my eyes last left it on my bedroom wall. Every single pixel that used to be a watery blue had suddenly recolored itself to a deep crimson - the very same crimson I had just wiped my hands clean of in the backyard. My arm hairs defy gravity for the first time in their life. I blink, and *B. waterways* returns to Father's iteration. No matter. A glimpse is all I need.

The morning of my Exhibition arrives quickly. Father and I don the ceremonial burgundy, and he doesn't even seem to contemplate asking me if I want to drive before he sits behind the steering wheel of the station wagon. Once again, my head finds its familiar resting place between the roof and the passenger seat's headrest, while my eyes silently observe the wheatfields blur together into their trademark soft yellow, #F9EB27.

Father maneuvers the station wagon into our assigned spot in the parking circle. I step out onto the street and prepare to simulate my typical brooding demeanor, but am surprised at how difficult it is. Excitement is not something I have experience concealing.

"Lucina," Father calls from behind me. "I just want you to know . . . " he trails off, a sheepish expression overcoming his pale face. "I just want you to know that whatever your iteration might be today, I will be proud of you."

"You'll regret saying that," I say without hesitation. Out of the corner of my eye, I see the edges of Father's lips descend simultaneously. I turn and walk into the Community Center before my lips do the opposite.

⊙

As I sit down, I catch Mr. Wingal's gaze from far behind me. He and the other Council members are the only ones who are aware of my assignment, which explains the fourteen other eyes I feel relentlessly dissecting me. I quickly make note of where they are all seated so I can compare their reactions after I present my Exhibition.

Father is one of the final residents to find his seat. The curvature of his spine is more pronounced than usual, a sign of his utter exhaustion. He does not look at me as he sits down.

The lights dim, and the standard message shows itself once again.

B. waterways. Iteration 4003030.
Designed by Resident 6C011C-2.

A millisecond after the message disappears, I focus my eyes directly forward and use them to project my iteration onto the screen, hearing a soft whrr come from my temples. I gently tap my right temple, freezing my iteration on the screen for the entire theater to see.

At first, I am unsure if I projected my iteration correctly, as an anticipatory silence still hangs in the dusty theater air. But then an array of sounds begin to surround me: sardonic chortles, frightened cries, uncensored gasps. The spotlight finds my seat, and I slowly rise. I thought I would be able to withstand any sort of audience-led persecution, but tears begin to nestle themselves inside my eyelids. A few seats to my left, a girl my age rolls her eyes and slightly shakes her head. *You dumbass*, she mouths to me with lips painted blue.

Father does not stand to hug me as I did for him. He remains seated, his lips slightly parted while he gazes forward in a petrified state. Realizing now that he would be the only one to support me, I bite my lip and cast my eyes to the side. *Tch. Why am I expecting to be rewarded after all my unrelenting bitterness towards him?*

There is only one thing remaining in the room that can console me, and I am still projecting it on the 1300 by 1300 theater screen. I consider terminating the projection, but that would be admitting defeat. I admire the way the crimson liquid splashes across the aqueducts the way the water once did. It was difficult for me to illustrate the heaviness of the liquid in only two dimensions, but I tried to minimize the number of waves in the river that runs underneath the aqueducts . . .

Lucina, this is called blood. B-L-O-O-D.

"Mother!" I exclaim to no one.

I collapse into my seat. There is no way for me to verify Mother's claim, but there is something about it that feels inherently *irrefutable*. I cannot stop myself from laughing. Infantile as it may seem, Mother's acceptance is the only thing that matters to me now.

And then I realize that the auditory assault towards me has completely halted. I look around and see that all of the other Community members are seated, their heads compressed between their palms. Their shouts are no longer directed at me.

"Father, is that you?"

"Mother, is that you?"

"What exactly is *blood*? Why is it like that?"

Gradually, like how the wind chooses which wheat stalks to shake first, the heads around the theater turn towards me. Their faces all have the same expression: awe.

"Lucina, you're a prophet!"

"Such beauty in elegance, such composure in form!"

"How did you do that? How did you know that replacing water with blood was the key?" an authoritative voice asks from behind me, urgency at its heels. Mr. Wingal.

I turn around, placing my knees on the seat—a difficult accomplishment in this dress.

Feeling confident as ever, I answer Mr. Wingal's question with one of my own. "What do you mean, 'key'?"

Mr. Wingal clears his throat and centers his lime green glasses. "Lucina, surely you must have wondered at some point what the whole point of *B. waterways* was. Having pixel-by-pixel iterations of the same image without an end goal serves no purpose. We at the Council observed your frustration building at each Exhibition. Allow me to explain why Exhibitions even exist to begin with.

"The creators of Damsel founded the Council to determine what constitutes the most objective definition of art. We know this is accomplished when the internal parent microchips—what you know as 'Mother'—are activated. This only happens whenever there is sufficient electrical current directed towards them. We Damselians are designed to allocate electrical current to our parent microchips only when we are inspired. Clearly, your iteration of *B. waterways* elicited enough inspiration to awaken several of the audience members' parent microchips."

I look around at the theater crowd again, then cross my arms. "If you knew this much about how we operate, how are you not frustrated time and time again after each Exhibition like I am?"

"All Councilmembers undergo a certain training before they are appointed. We learn that when Damsel was created, everything was generated based on a template. Damsel as we know it is just one random variation of this template. Certain new features were added, like blood underneath the wheat stalks, and certain features were removed—water being the most notable. Everything about Damsel, from the parent microchips to *B. waterways* itself, is to accomplish one goal: to determine which environment is best suited for inspiration."

Mr. Wingal nods with a sort of acknowledgement towards me that I never thought he would be capable of. "No one knows who designed us, or how they were able to codify inspiration as electrical current," he says. "But do not dwell on that for now. Look around—you have enriched the Community's lives with a beauty they never even thought as possible."

He was right. The same Community members who had crucified me seconds ago were now glowing with an undeniable happiness. I allow myself a smile and look above the crowd at my iteration on the screen one final time. It does not fascinate me anymore. Interchanging water for blood is too simple of a transformation to be called "art." *My parent microchip must require a lower amount of electrical current to activate it. Inspiration comes easily to me, but leaves just as quick. Damn whoever programmed me into this vicious cycle.*

I turn to Father. He is sitting complacently in his seat, eyes still fixated on the screen.

"Father." He pivots his head slightly towards me. "Did you hear a voice inside you when you saw my iteration?" I ask.

"A voice . . ." Father goes quiet. I have never seen him this calm. There is no more urge to appease hiding beneath his beady eyes.

"Lucina . . ." he says slowly. "Today, you allowed me to fulfill my function as your Father. I serve no more purpose. You have made me undeniably proud."

A soft smile rests on Father's face, and his eyes go still. I watch as the soft light behind his pupils gradually dims. My eyes instinctively avert themselves, and they find my hands. I rub my fingertips together, still flecked with the dry blood from digging beneath the wheatfields.

CONTRIBUTORS

Fayaway & Hermester Barrington

Hermester is a retired archivist, a rogue protozoologist, and a deliberately genre ignorant artist, whose ficciones have recently appeared in *Fate Magazine*, *Mythaxis*, and *Robot Butt*. Fayaway, who usually works in ephemeral media only, is a gardener, urban archaeologist, and on again, off again member of the postfolkpunk group Medusa's Greatgreatgranddaughters. This is the first of their joint projects to be published; their next project is the book *Munchausen by Proxy—A Child's Guide to Getting There First* (Golden Press Books, forthcoming Autumn 2023).

David Bradley

David Bradley is a freelance writer with one non-fiction book (*The Historic Murder Trial of George Crawford*) to his credit. His short stories and poetry have appeared in *Broken Pencil*, *The Adirondack Review*, *Down in the Dirt*, *Main Street Rag*, *The South Carolina Review*, and *Pennsylvania English*. He has spent a dozen years as a newspaper reporter and columnist in Northern Virginia.

Daniel David Froid

Daniel David Froid is a writer who lives in Arizona and has published fiction in *Post Road*, *Black Warrior Review*, *Lightspeed*, and elsewhere.

A. P. Howell

A. P. Howell's jobs have spanned the alphabet from archivist to webmaster. She lives with her husband, their two kids, and a pair of rambunctious puppies. Her short fiction has appeared in various venues, including *ParSec*, *Martian, Dread Space* (Shacklebound Books), *Bicycles & Broomsticks* (Microcosm Publishing), and *Darkness Blooms* (The Dread Machine).

She sometimes hangs out online on Mastodon (wandering. shop/@aphowell) and her homepage is aphowell.com.

Erik Kollmer

This is Erik Kollmer's fiction debut. He tells stories with data for a living. That's what he tells himself anyways. He feels that his data storytelling work does not allow him full narrative control, so his fiction seeks to reclaim that.

Kiya Nicoll

Kiya Nicoll is a writer, poet, and artist living in a New England oak grove. They dabble in a wide variety of assorted obsessions when permitted to do so by the children, the cats, and the limitations of physical embodiment. Their work has previously appeared in magazines including the *Escape Pod* podcast and several anthologies, most recently *Bioluminescent: A Lunarpunk Anthology*.

They can be found at kiyanicoll.com, on Twitter at kiya_nicoll, and in the Fediverse at @gehennan@wandering.shop.

J. P. Oakes

J. P. Oakes is a writer and creative director living on Long Island. His debut novel, *City of Iron and Dust* is available from Titan Books, and according to *Publishers Weekly* "offers lovers of the bloody and fantastical plenty to enjoy."

He can be found online at jpoakeswrites.wordpress.com.

Roni Stinger

Roni Stinger's fiction has recently been published in *Dark Matter Magazine, Unnerving Magazine*, and *Rewired: Divergent Perspectives in Horror*, among others.

Find her online at www.ronistinger.com.

Jason Washer

Jason Washer lives in New Hampshire and divides his time between caring for his family, running a small business, and writing stories late into the night at his kitchen table. His work has appeared in the *No Sleep Podcast, Mystery Tribune, Theme of Absence, Bards and Sages Quarterly*, and in the anthology *In Darkness, Delight: Fear the Future.*

Find him on the web at www.jasonwasher.net.

Eric Witchey

Eric Witchey has sold stories under several names and in 12 genres. His tales have been translated into multiple languages, and his credits include over 160 stories, including 5 novels and two collections. He has taught over 200 conference seminars and classes at 2 universities and a community college. His work has received recognition from New Century Writers, Writers of the Future, Writer's Digest, Independent Publisher Book Awards, International Book Awards, The Eric Hoffer Prose Award Program, Short Story America, the Irish Aeon Awards, and other organizations.

Eric Witchey's How-to articles have appeared in *The Writer Magazine*, *Writer's Digest Magazine*, and other print and online magazines.

PAMELA COLMAN SMITH

The tarot images in this issue of Arcana are from the deck illustrated by Pamela Colman Smith. It was released in 1909 as the Rider-Waite deck (so named, at that time, in reference to its publisher, William Rider & Son). It remains the most influential and widely used tarot deck. While the impetus for the deck came from Arthur Edward Waite, Colman Smith was responsible for the iconography of the cards.

Pamela Colman Smith also illustrated over twenty books, wrote two collections of Jamaican folklore, edited two magazines, and ran the Green Sheaf Press, a small press devoted to women writers. She continued to write and illustrate throughout her life.

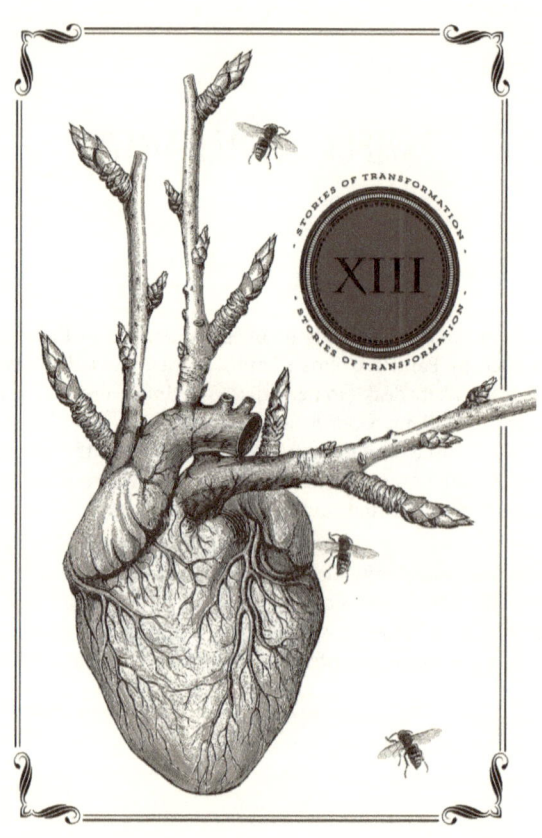

STORIES OF TRANSFORMATION

XIII

STORIES OF TRANSFORMATION

XIII

The thirteenth Tarot card is Death, and he is a symbol not of the end, but of transformation and rebirth. This is the genesis and root of *Thirteen: Stories of Transformation*. The twenty-eight authors of this collection are voices—new and old—who are not afraid to explore what comes next. Whether it be a life after death, a life without love, a life filled with hunger, or the life shared by a ghost. These are stories of the weird, the mythic, the fantastic, the futuristic, the supernatural, and the horrific.

With stories by Liz Argall • M. David Blake • Richard Bowes • George Cotronis • Amanda C. Davis • Julie C. Day • Jetse de Vries • Jennifer Giesbrecht • Daryl Gregory • Rik Hoskin • Rebecca Kuder • Claude Lalumière • Marc Levinthal • Grá Linnaea • Alex Dally MacFarlane • Juli Mallett • Lyn McConchie • Fiona Moore • Gregory L. Norris • Adrienne J. Odasso • Cat Rambo • Andrew Penn Romine • David Tallerman • Tais Teng Richard Thomas • Fran Wilde • A. C. Wise • Christie Yant

Edited by Mark Teppo.

Available at independent bookstores everywhere.

http://www.underlandpress.com

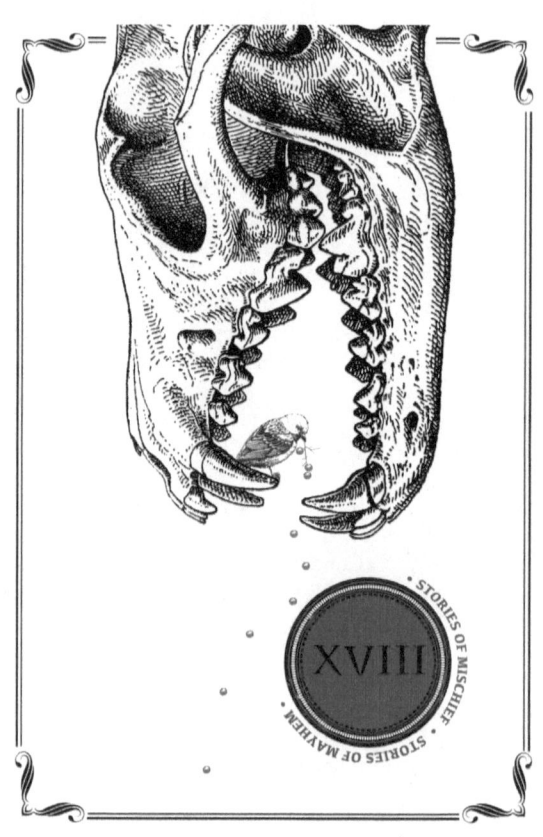

XVIII

• STORIES OF MISCHIEF •
• STORIES OF MAYHEM •

XVIII

The eighteenth Tarot card is the Moon, and those who raise their arms to her know she offers Mercy and Severity in equal measure. This is the great river at night, where wolves howl and all doors are open. All futures are possible, and every truth is elusive. This is the source and passion of *Eighteen: Stories of Mischief & Mayhem*. These twenty-four stories from voices—old and new—celebrate the inevitability of fate, the horror of prophecy, and the shivering delight of not knowing what comes next.

Cross over the threshold with us, and explore the strange, the weird, and the fantastic. Do not fear what lies ahead. It is the same as what came before. The only difference is you. This is *Eighteen*, and nothing will be the same.

With stories by Forrest Aguirre • Darin Bradley • Christopher East • Scott Edelman • Nicole Feldringer • Ben Gamblin • Ingrid Garcia • A. P. Howell • Emma Johnson-Rivard • E. E. King • Jessie Kwak • Shannon Lawrence • Gerri Leen • Mark Mills • Christi Nogle Tammie Painter • Josh Rountree • Erica Sage • Lorraine Schein • J. Dee Stanley • Richard Thomas • John Waterfall • Wendy N. Wagner • Todd Zack

Edited by Mark Teppo.

Available at independent bookstores everywhere.

http://www.underlandpress.com